Jim Henson's™

FRANKEN-SCI HIGH

HIGH

BEWARE OF THE GIANT BRAIN!

Remembering when I made up stories for you as kids
and how you were my first audience.
This is for you, Matt and Rennie. —M. Y.

SIMON SPOTLIGHT
An imprint of Simon & Schuster Children's Publishing Division
1230 Avenue of the Americas, New York, New York 10020
This Simon Spotlight hardcover edition July 2020
© 2020 The Jim Henson Company. JIM HENSON'S mark & logo, FRANKEN-SCI HIGH mark & logo, characters, and elements are trademarks of The Jim Henson Company. All Rights Reserved.
All rights reserved, including the right of reproduction in whole or in part in any form.
SIMON SPOTLIGHT and colophon are registered trademarks of Simon & Schuster, Inc.
For information about special discounts for bulk purchases, please contact Simon & Schuster Special Sales at 1-866-506-1949 or business@simonandschuster.com.
Manufactured in the United States of America 0620 BVG 10 9 8 7 6 5 4 3 2 1
ISBN 978-1-4814-9140-2 (hc)
ISBN 978-1-4814-9139-6 (pbk)
ISBN 978-1-4814-9141-9 (eBook)

Jim Henson's™ FRANKEN-SCI HIGH

BEWARE OF THE GIANT BRAIN!

CREATED BY **MARK YOUNG**
TEXT WRITTEN BY **TRACEY WEST**
ILLUSTRATED BY **MARIANO EPELBAUM**

Simon Spotlight
New York London Toronto Sydney New Delhi

CHAPTER 1

A
Shocking Morning

"Students of Franken-Sci High! It has come to my attention that many of you are still asleep after last night's cast party. Please report to the cafeteria right away. The school has an important announcement to make!"

Newton Warp groaned as he woke up to the voice of Headmistress Mumtaz, which seemed to be shouting into his ear. Then he felt something tickle the inside of his ear. A tiny, mechanical, fly-like creature flew out of it and left the room through the crack on top of the door. It was quickly followed by another mechanical fly that came from the bottom bunk, where Newton's roommate slept.

Newton hung upside down from the top bunk and gazed at his roommate, Higgy, who was oozing out of bed. His gooey green body, made entirely of protoplasm, was tucked inside a pair of flannel

pajamas with rubber chicken drawings on them.

"Why is she making us go to the cafeteria?" Newton moaned. "It's the weekend!"

"You know Mumtaz," Higgy replied. "She loves an assembly."

Newton quickly hopped off the bed. "And why was that announcement so loud? It felt like it was right in my ear."

"Oh, those are her fly drones," Higgy explained. "She has a whole horde of them that she can target to reach each student at the school. Each one has a powerful micro speaker inside. Pretty impressive, but usually they're reserved for emergencies."

"Well, I need more sleep," Newton said with a yawn. "I hope this announcement is worth it."

"We'd better get dressed before she sends her scream-ing cyborgs," Higgy warned. "They're a lot louder!"

Newton knew that listening to Higgy was a good idea, and he slipped on jeans and a lime-green T-shirt with the school's motto on it: "A Brain Is a Terrible Thing to Waste . . . Unless You Can Grow Another One."

He yawned again. It wasn't just that he'd been up last night, celebrating with the rest of the cast of *Frankenstein: The Musical*. Even after he'd climbed into bed, well after midnight, he hadn't been able to

sleep. His mind had been racing with the news he'd heard earlier that night.

Newton was a new student at Franken-Sci High. The school was filled with plenty of unusual students: robots, Higgy, and even a kid who was a brain in a jar, Odifin Pinkwad. Newton looked like an ordinary human, but he was probably the most unusual student of them all.

His friends Shelly and Theremin had discovered him in the Brain Bank of the school library with no memory of who he was or where he'd come from, with a school ID with his name on it, and a bar code permanently imprinted on the sole of his left foot.

In the last few weeks, Newton had learned some things. He had uncovered strange memories of being hatched from a giant egg. He had extra-human abilities: his fingertips and toes were sticky and helped him climb walls; he could camouflage himself when he was in danger; he could sprout gills and breathe underwater; and he could make himself look like other humans if he wanted to.

He had also learned from Professor Hercule Flubitus that he and Shelly were very important to the future of the school, but Professor Flubitus hadn't told them why. Even so, they were so important that Flubitus had

traveled from the future to protect them.

And last night Flubitus had told Newton the most amazing thing of all: Newton had a relative living at the school! When Newton had heard this, he'd been shocked and quiet. But the more he thought about it, the more he wanted to scream and jump and laugh and cry all at the same time. Shelly and Theremin and Higgy were awesome friends, but it still bothered Newton that he had no idea where he was from, or even if he had a family. Professor Flubitus's news was the best news ever.

But the flustered professor had refused to give up the identity of the relative to Newton. And Newton had gone to the cast party, where they'd eaten lots of pizza and freeze-dried potato chips, and had danced and sung songs from the school musical, and it just hadn't been the place to talk about what Flubitus had said. So Newton had been up all night, wondering who this relative might be.

Was it one of the students? Would it be somebody nice, like Tori Twitcher? Or somebody not so nice, like Mimi Crowninshield?

Was it one of the professors? Maybe the loud-and-large monster maker, Professor Gertrude Leviathan? Or Professor Wells, who was stuck between two

dimensions? Newton could imagine having some fun adventures with those two.

Or maybe it was somebody on the staff? He hoped it wasn't Stubbins Crouch, the school custodian. But there were some nice cooks in the cafeteria. If one of them was his mom, maybe she would make him cookies or something. Or mac-and-cheese sandwiches. That was one of his favorite foods. . . .

"Better hurry up, Newton. We don't want to miss anything," Higgy said. He had changed into his usual outfit: a heavy coat, rubber boots and gloves, a wool cap, glasses, and bandages wrapping his face. Newton didn't mind hanging around with a kid made of green goo, but Higgy's outfit made it easier for other kids to accept him.

"Right," Newton answered. "I just need to use the bathroom."

"That's one thing I don't mind about not being human," Higgy said. "Your waste excretion functions are so inefficient."

"Well, I'm not exactly human either," Newton reminded him.

A few minutes later the roommates were walking from their dorm room to the school's main building. Because the school was located somewhere in the middle of the Bermuda Triangle, the air was hot and

moist. Palm trees and brightly colored flowers grew along the path, and birds chattered and swooped among the vegetation, along with the security and weather drones.

Once Newton and Higgy were inside the building, the transport tube sucked them up to the fourth floor. It was crowded with sleepy-looking kids who didn't seem happy about Mumtaz's early-morning wake-up announcement.

"I'm going to the yogurt bar," Higgy announced, and Newton nodded. Something about being made of protoplasm made Higgy crave things that were creamy and gooey.

Newton and Higgy got into the food line. A server wearing a thick white glove placed a mug filled with a steaming blue concoction onto Newton's tray.

"What's this?" Newton asked.

"This morning's special from the Bio-Voltage Lab," the server replied. "Guaranteed to wake you up."

"Sounds perfect!" Newton said, and he made his way through the crowds of mad-scientist students until he found Shelly and Theremin. Shelly had a mug of the steaming blue stuff in front of her, and Theremin didn't have anything, because robots don't eat.

"Hey, guys!" Newton said, sliding into his seat. "As

soon as Higgy gets here with his yogurt, I've got really exciting news to tell you."

"Great!" Shelly replied. "But first you need to know that—"

"Ow!" Newton cried. He'd picked up his mug, and a quick jolt of electricity had zapped him.

"I tried to warn you," Shelly said. "The cafeteria staff thought shocking us awake this morning was a good idea. The concoction inside is pretty good, though. Just use this."

She handed him a straw. "It's made of fruit leather," she said. "You can eat it when you're done."

"Thanks," Newton said. "The shock wasn't so bad. At least I'm awake now."

"How could you be tired? My circuits are still charged up from last night," Theremin chimed in. "It felt so great to be onstage! And seeing my dad there, that was awesome."

Newton nodded. Theremin's father, Professor Rozika, was a robotics professor who had been pretty hard on Theremin ever since he'd created him. But things were getting better between them.

Higgy slid up to the table and plopped down a tray piled with bowls of yogurt.

"Hungry?" Shelley asked.

"I expended a great deal of energy onstage last night," Higgy replied. "Not to mention at the party."

"Yeah, you never stopped dancing," Newton agreed.

A group of kids who Newton didn't know stopped by the table and stood next to Shelly.

"Shelly, you were amazing last night," said a girl with purple hair.

"Yeah, you made me believe you were Dr. Frankenstein!" said a boy wearing pants and a shirt made of aluminum foil.

"Thanks," Shelly replied. "The whole cast was great, right?"

"I played the cook," Theremin piped up.

"Um, sure," said the purple-haired girl. "It's just, you know, Shelly was *electrifying*!"

"You're a superstar now, Shelly," Higgy said. Then he burped, and the group of kids walked away.

Shelly blushed. "We were all good," she said. "Theremin, you were hilarious, and Newton, you were a great head villager, and Higgy, you brought dignity and humanity to Frankenstein's monster."

"I did indeed," Higgy agreed.

"Anyway. Newton, you had some news?" Shelly asked.

"Oh, right," Newton said. "After the play Flubitus

told me I have a relative at this school!"

Shelly gasped. "No way!"

"Fantastic, roomie!" Higgy said.

"Is it me?" Theremin asked. "Maybe we're brothers!"

"I don't think so," Newton said. "But I'm not sure. Right after he told me, Flubitus clammed up. He said he couldn't say who. It's so frustrating!"

"If Flubitus won't tell you, we'll find out on our own," Shelly promised. "We can come up with a plan, right after—"

"Attention, students!"

The voice of Headmistress Mumtaz blared through the cafeteria. A giant hologram of her head appeared in the space and began to spin around. With her sharp nose, orange-and-purple-streaked hair, and thin face, she had always reminded Newton of one of the birds on the island.

"First, I'd like to thank the cast and crew of *Frankenstein: The Musical* for their wonderful performance last night," she began, and everyone applauded. "And now it's time for our next event to show off the talents of our student body: the annual Brilliant Brains Trivia Competition!"

A cheer went up among the students, and before Newton could ask his friends *What's that?* the

headmistress launched into an explanation.

"Our faculty has spent the last year coming up with mind-bending trivia questions in a variety of categories, including the four major areas of mad-scientist study. The four areas of study are Unconventional Chemistry, Heretical Electricity, Irregular Biology, and Extra-Theoretical Physics," she explained. "Contestants will be eliminated one by one until the most Brilliant Brain is crowned!"

An even bigger cheer went up.

"This year's winner will receive a full set of the Encyclopedia of Mad Scientists—all seven hundred and fifty-three gilded volumes, the perfect accent to any mad scientist's lair," Mumtaz went on. "As well as the micro-digital form for convenience."

"That is a spectacular prize!" Higgy said, nudging Newton.

"And as an extraspecial treat, there will also be a giant holographic statue of the winner projected in a special place of honor in the school's Center Court for one week to commemorate the victory," she said. "So start studying, students. The Brilliant Brains Trivia Competition is three weeks from today. May the best brain win!"

The giant hologram of her face flickered and then

disappeared. Everyone in the cafeteria started talking at once.

Newton heard Mimi Crowninshield's voice above the others. "Nobody else should even bother entering, because I am going to win!" she bragged.

Shelly rolled her eyes. "Shouldn't she be disqualified from all school competitions after she tried to sabotage the musical?"

"Her family sponsors the trivia competition," Higgy reminded her. "No Mimi, no contest."

"Now that Father has removed any programming that punishes me for being smart, I might just enter," Theremin said. "I bet I'll ace it!"

At that moment a brain in a jar of liquid rolled up on a small wheeled table, accompanied by a tall, skinny boy with greasy black hair. The brain was Odifin Pinkwad, and the boy was his assistant, Rotwang Conkell.

Odifin's voice came through a speaker attached to the front of his jar. "Ah, Newton, I suppose you're going to cheat your way through the competition, aren't you?" he accused.

"What do you mean?" Newton asked.

"I've had my visual processors on you," Odifin said. "Most of the time you behave like a brainless dolt. But when it's time to take a test, you're suddenly a

genius! I know you've found some sophisticated cheating technique that the professors can't detect. Well, I'm warning you. Don't try cheating your way through this competition. Because *I* am going to win, fair and square!"

"Yeah, he's the fairest and squarest," Rotwang said.

"I don't cheat," Newton replied, but it wasn't exactly true. One of the weird things he had discovered about himself since waking up at Franken-Sci High was that when he heard the words "noodle noggin," he became a genius for a little while. But he tried to only activate that ability when he really needed to.

"Hmph!" Odifin snorted. "Remember, I am the all-seeing Odifin Pinkwad!"

"Too bad your eyes are stuck in a jar!" Theremin said. "Now get out of here and leave my friend alone."

"Come, Rotwang. Let's leave these losers to themselves," Odifin said, and he rolled away, with Rotwang loping behind him.

"What a jerk," Theremin said.

"Aw, I don't know," Newton said. "I mean, he was kind of right about my noodle noggin thing. Besides, it can't be easy being a brain in a jar."

"You're so sweet, Newton," Shelly said. "But Odifin makes it hard on himself. I tried being nice to him when

he first came to this school, and he's only ever been mean."

"Yeah, don't feel sorry for that guy," Theremin said.

Newton watched Odifin roll away. He and Rotwang sat a table by themselves, like they always did. Odifin usually floated in his jar while Rotwang stuffed his face with more plates of food than anyone else in the cafeteria—even Higgy and Hector Bovina, who was rumored to have once traveled to the eighteenth dimension and come back with an extra stomach.

Newton looked around at his friends, and looked back at Odifin.

I think I do feel sorry for him, Newton thought. *I may not know who I am, or have any memories. But all of my new memories are pretty good ones! What good memories does poor Odifin have?*

CHAPTER 2

Twenty Brains Are Better Than One

"What does that walking garbage can know, anyway?" Odifin said to Rotwang as he eyed Theremin across the cafeteria. "My eyes may be here in this jar, but they have quite a range of motion on their eyestalks. More than a normal human. See?" Odifin demonstrated by wiggling his eyeballs back and forth on their stalks.

"Nice trick, Odifin," Rotwang agreed, stuffing a sausage into his mouth.

"And I *will* keep watch on Newton," Odifin continued. "Nothing about him makes sense. The official story is that he was discovered in the Brain Bank with amnesia. Most of the time he acts like he doesn't know a thing. And then sometimes he's a genius! It doesn't smell right."

"Yeah, smell," Rotwang said as he sniffed his stack of pancakes. Then he stabbed them with his fork.

Odifin's visual processors gazed at Newton, who was

laughing at something Shelly was saying. He felt a pang of—jealousy, maybe?

No, not that! Odifin thought. *It's just baffling! Nothing about him makes sense!*

What confused Odifin most is how quickly Newton had made friends after coming to the school. For Odifin, the transition hadn't been so easy. He'd been homeschooled by his mom, a brilliant mad scientist in her own right, for years. She'd taught him silly songs to remember complicated things: *Don't be a fool! You need more than one atom to make a molecule.* . . . And she'd always told him he was the smartest boy in the whole world, and how much she loved him, and how proud she was of him.

Odifin had been happy then. His mom had been his whole world. Sure, he knew that they looked different from each other—she had a body made of flesh and bones and hair and other things that he didn't have— but they loved each other.

Then, one day, his mom had told him it was time for him to go out into the world. She was sending him to Franken-Sci High. Odifin had begged and pleaded to stay home, but his mom had insisted.

"You need to meet people and make friends, Odifin," she had said. "I can't keep you all to myself.

And there are some things I just can't teach you."

So Odifin had been sent through a portal to Franken-Sci High, but meeting people and making friends hadn't been easy. It wasn't even that kids had stared at him or made fun of him. Most of them hadn't even realized he was a kid, just like them. At first many of them thought he was a piece of equipment, or an experiment.

It didn't help that his mom had arranged for Rotwang to go to the school too. While other students at Franken-Sci High were from mad-scientist families, Rotwang was from a long line of assistants. Assistants usually went to their own school, the Igor Institute, but Rotwang had been sent to help Odifin do the things that Odifin couldn't do by himself—such as charge the battery on his recently motorized table, or reboot his sense processor when it messed up. Rotwang used to have to push Odifin's rolling table around campus too, until recently, when Odifin had had it altered so he could move the table's wheels just by thinking about it. That had given him some freedom, at least. But not much.

Rotwang was useful, but he didn't talk much, and he and Odifin had nothing in common. And Rotwang seemed to repel the other mad scientists; most of them thought it was beneath them to be seen with an assistant.

The only student who'd ever tried to be nice to him

was Shelly Ravenholt, and his processors had picked up the look of pity in her eyes, and that had been too much for Odifin.

"Why don't you go hang out with your monster misfits instead?" he'd said when Shelly had invited him to go to movie night with her and Theremin once. Shelly had looked sad and gone off, and Odifin had instantly regretted it. He actually thought the little monsters Shelly rescued or repaired were cute. But he couldn't stand her pity.

I'd rather be hated than pitied, Odifin had thought, more than once, and with his razor wit and inflated ego, he'd done a pretty good job of getting kids to hate him.

The only problem was that he knew how disappointed his mom would be if she knew he didn't have any friends. So whenever they video-chatted, he lied.

"Oh yes, um, Salton Pepper and I went to the Airy Café last night," he'd said once, making up a name on the spot. "It was very fun."

"See, Odifin, I just knew you'd fit right in at school," his mom had said. "Soon you'll be the most popular boy at Franken-Sci High!"

Odifin didn't have the heart to tell her the truth. It was the first time he had failed at something she'd asked him to do, and the first time he had lied to her.

Determined to figure out how to be popular, he'd started scanning social media sites. He'd done an analysis of the teens who were trending with the most followers and hits. They were the best-looking, or the richest, or the ones with popular songs or who starred in movies.

That's why Odifin had tried out for the school musical, hoping that it would help him become popular. But it hadn't worked. Shelly had become an instant celebrity, but nothing had happened to him.

That's okay, Odifin thought. *Because now I have another chance, thanks to the Brilliant Brains Trivia Competition! If anyone is a natural to win, it's me. And when that holographic statue of me goes up in the Center Court, I* will *be the most popular kid in school!*

"Rotwang, here is today's plan," Odifin said now. "We have a free day, so let's go to the library Brain Bank. I want to study for the trivia contest."

Rotwang frowned. "Do we have to go to the library? You said I could play video games today."

"I know, Rotwang, but this is important," Odifin said. "I need to study if I'm going to win the contest."

"You're already smart," Rotwang said, and Odifin suspected that his assistant was just buttering him up.

"I need to be the smartest," Odifin said. "The smartest brain in the world! And I need you to help me plug into the ports in the Brain Bank."

Rotwang sighed. "Yes, Odifin," he said.

"Excellent!" Odifin said. "Now hurry up and stuff that food down your throat. We need to get going."

Rotwang ate as fast as someone can eat a dozen pancakes, a pound of bacon, a whole cantaloupe, and two dozen crispy hash browns.

"Honestly, Rotwang, I don't know how you are so skinny," Odifin said. "It's physically impossible."

Rotwang shrugged. "Genes, I guess."

"What does an assistant know about genes?" Odifin snapped. "Come on. Let's get to the Brain Bank."

The Brain Bank was Odifin's favorite place in the school, probably because everybody in it looked like him. The room was filled with nothing but brains floating in jars of liquid. These brains couldn't see or talk like Odifin could—his mom had said that he, Odifin, had been created using much more advanced technology than those in the Brain Bank. But students could plug their tablets into ports on the brain jars and download information to help them study. Odifin didn't use a tablet; anything electronic he used for studying was plugged directly into a port on his jar, and shot right into his brain.

Once they were in the Brain Bank, Odifin asked, "Where should we start, Rotwang?" Rotwang just shrugged, so Odifin continued. "Mumtaz said the first trivia category will be Unconventional Chemistry. So let's find the brain of Elvira Mixenhooper. She's one of the greatest unconventional chemists of all time."

Rotwang slowly walked around and squinted at the brains. "Is it this one?"

Odifin rolled over to him. "No, that's not Elvira Mixenhooper. That's Elvena Mixelheimer, a molecular time travel pioneer! Find me Elvira!"

Rotwang moved down the row. "Here she is."

Odifin rolled over to the brain of Elvira Mixenhooper. It looked like an ordinary brain, but Odifin knew that it contained a wealth of information that he wouldn't be able to find in any book.

"Plug me in!" Odifin commanded.

Rotwang quickly attached a connector to Elvira's port, and plugged the other end into Odifin's jar, and Odifin felt his nerve endings tingle. Then he heard a female voice in his brain.

Hello, young man. Or should I say, young brain?

"I am Odifin Pinkwad," he replied.

How is it that you are on wheels, Odifin? That looks like a lot of fun.

"It's a long story," Odifin replied. "Right now I need you to tell me everything you know about Unconventional Chemistry.

Certainly, Elvira said. *It's been a long time since any student has connected with me. Although, I do hope that you will tell me about those wheels of yours when I'm through.*

Then Elvira began a lecture on Unconventional Chemistry. Unlike other kids, Odifin didn't need to take notes. The information went right into his memory banks, and he was able to call up those memories at

will. His mom said that was one reason why he was the smartest boy in the world.

Elvira went on and on about her experiments and inventions. Plant food that helped carrots grow to be twelve feet long. Perfume that changed the appearance of the person wearing it. Peanut butter that was altered to taste like jelly, and jelly that was altered to taste like peanut butter.

Elvira had a lot to say, and Odifin absorbed every word. After a few hours, Elvira gave no sign that she was going to stop anytime soon.

"Excuse me," Odifin said. "How much longer will this take?"

It all depends on how much you want to know, Odifin, Elvira replied. *I have at least forty-two more hours of information for you. And I'm not the only Unconventional Chemistry expert in here. There's Klaus Widdershins, and Romeo Yolando, and—*

"I understand," Odifin said. At this rate, Odifin realized, it would take him forever to get ready for the contest! But there was nothing he could do about that. "Continue, please."

Elvira started to lecture again, but a squeaking sound interrupted her. Odifin looked away from Elvira to see Rotwang drawing on one of the brain jars with a marker.

"Rotwang, what are you doing?" Odifin asked. Then he noticed that his assistant had drawn eyeglasses and a mustache onto the jar of the school's first Harnessing the Power of Lightning professor. "Are you serious? Stop that!"

"But . . . I'm bored," Rotwang complained. "There's nothing to do in here."

"Go get a book from the library to read," Odifin snapped. "But come right back. After I'm done with Elvira, I need you to hook me up to Ignatius Nakamura. He's known as the father of Heretical Electricity."

"Books are boring," Rotwang grumbled, but he slunk away and came back a few minutes later with a copy of *How to Overthrow Your Overlords in Ten Easy Steps*.

"Thank you, Elvira," Odifin said. "I need to move on now."

You're welcome, Odifin. Now if you could tell me more about those wheels of yours—

"Rotwang, connect me to Ignatius, now!" Odifin commanded.

Rotwang removed the connector and followed Odifin as he rolled over to Ignatius Nakamura's jar. Rotwang had drawn an eyepatch over one of the floating eyeballs and a grinning mouth with huge front teeth.

"Really, Rotwang?" Odifin asked.

Rotwang just shrugged and plugged in the connector, and Odifin heard the voice of Ignatius.

It said, *Excuse me, young man! Can you please clean my jar? I can't see out of my right eye!*

Odifin sighed and thought, *Once I'm popular, I'll have friends to help me out, for once. No more Rotwang!*

CHAPTER **3**

Mysterious Mumtaz

"Peewee! Stop chewing on Theremin's leg!" Shelly scolded. "Bad monster!"

A furry blue monster that was the size of a small cat froze mid-munch, and then scurried to hide behind the leaves of a potted plant. Newton, Shelly, Theremin, and Higgy were in Shelly's mostly secret animal rescue lab in the school basement. Headmistress Mumtaz knew about it, and so did Professor Gertrude Leviathan, who taught monster-making. Shelly was great at making monsters, but she also loved to bio-upgrade animals that had been injured, and then release them into the wild.

The animals currently living in the lab were: an iguana with a robotic tail that could warn him when a dangerous animal was sneaking up behind him; a fish in a glass bubble equipped with mechanical legs; and Peewee, the furry blue monster that had once followed Shelly home when she was on vacation.

Shelly had equipped the lab with artificial sunli
a small pond, and plants from the animals' nat
environments.

"It's a bit stuffy down here," Higgy complained. "
there a reason why we're meeting in Shelly's lab?"

"Privacy," Shelly answered. "If Flubitus won't tell
Newton who his relative is, there must be a reason. So
if we're going to find out who it is, we need to keep our
search a secret. Maybe Newton's relative doesn't want
him to find out either."

That thought hadn't occurred to Newton yet, and it
made him sad. "I hope whoever is related to me will,
you know, be happy about it," he said.

"I know I would be," Theremin said.

"Secrecy it is, then," Higgy said. "I hope you understand if I unwind, then." Without waiting for an answer,
he took off his hat and goggles, unwrapped the bandages around his face, and then replaced his goggles.
"That's better."

"Good!" said Newton.

"Great. Okay, so let's start with what we know,"
Shelly said, and she tapped the screen of her tablet. A
holographic list projected into the air:

**1. NEWTON DOESN'T KNOW WHERE HE CAME
FROM.**

2. NEWTON HAS A BAR CODE ON HIS FOOT.

3. NEWTON HAS SUPERHUMAN ABILITIES.

4. FLUBITUS TRAVELED THROUGH TIME TO MAKE SURE NEWTON STAYS SAFE.

5. FLUBITUS SAYS NEWTON HAS A RELATIVE IN THE SCHOOL.

"Did I forget anything?" Shelly asked.

"You forget to mention that Newton has an awesome friend named Theremin," Theremin replied.

"And a roommate named Higgy," Higgy added.

"Those things are true, but they're not relevant to the problem we're trying to solve," Shelly said. "If Newton has family in the school, maybe they have amnesia too. Or special abilities. Or maybe they look like Newton."

"Looks don't necessarily mean anything," Higgy said. "I don't look a thing like my brother. He's chartreuse, and I'm lime green."

"Isn't the best way to tell if humans are related is to test their DNA?" Theremin asked.

"Of course!" Shelly and Higgy shouted.

Newton frowned. "What's DNA?"

Theremin's eyes flashed blue as he accessed his data banks. "'DNA' stands for 'deoxyribonucleic acid,'" he responded. "It's, like, the stuff in your cells that contains all your genetic information—the things you inherited

from your parents that determine how you look and how your body works."

"Right," Higgy said. "And anyone who is genetically related to you will share some of the same DNA."

Newton's mind was whirring. This DNA stuff meant that he could know for sure who his relative was. No guessing.

"How do you look at someone's DNA if it's in their cells? That sounds painful," Newton said.

"You can test for DNA using a strand of hair, or saliva," Theremin said. "The test itself is complicated, but collecting DNA is pretty easy."

"I could sneak into everyone's rooms and steal their toothbrushes," Higgy offered.

"That would be hundreds of toothbrushes—and gross," Shelly said. "Besides, DNA testing is expensive. Unless . . . maybe we could use the school's lab."

"That lab is off-limits to all students except for seniors," Theremin pointed out. "Mumtaz would never let us use it."

"What about Mumtaz?" Newton asked. "I mean, we haven't asked her yet who my relative is. If Flubitus knows, she must know."

"And if she doesn't, she could arrange to have everyone's DNA tested for us," Shelly said. "It's worth a try!"

"Definitely. Let's go talk to her!" Newton said.

After making sure all of Shelly's creatures had fresh water and food, they left the rescue lab and made their way up to Mumtaz's office.

"Wait a minute. It's the weekend," Newton said. "She won't be there."

"She's *always* there," Theremin said. "She says that she's headmistress twenty-four hours a day, seven days a week."

Newton knocked on her office door. A tiny drone floated down in front of them and scanned each one of their faces. Then her voice came through a speaker.

"Come in, Newton, Shelly, Theremin, and Higgy."

They entered and sat in the metal chairs across from her desk. As usual, the headmistress wore clothes as colorful as her orange-and-purple-streaked hair. Her fuchsia blouse had bright green leopard spots on it, and she wore a chunky necklace with alternating blue and red beads.

"What can I do for you?" Mumtaz asked.

"You can DNA test everyone at Franken-Sci High for us," Theremin blurted out.

Mumtaz raised her eyebrows. "And why would I need to do that?"

"Professor Flubitus told me that I have a relative here at the school," Newton explained, "but he wouldn't tell

32

me who, so I'm trying to find out. Unless you know?"

The eyes of the headmistress flickered for a nanosecond. "I know nothing about this," she said. "Perhaps Flubitus was confused. Time travel has a way of turning your brain inside out."

Newton's heart sank. "I don't think he would say that if it weren't true," he said. "He knows how much it means to me to find my family."

"Well, even if he is right," Mumtaz began, "I'm afraid DNA testing every biological unit in this school is simply not possible. First off, it's a very time-consuming, expensive process."

"We'll raise the money," Shelly said.

"Yes, we could do a bake sale!" Higgy offered. "Or perhaps a yogurt sale. Mmm, yogurt."

Mumtaz shook her head. "That's not the only reason. Collecting DNA from students has been banned for decades, ever since Horatio Doppelganger tried to use students' DNA to create a clone army of mad scientists to do his bidding."

"I've never heard of Horatio Doppelganger," Shelly said.

"He's been erased from all history books, because we don't want any students trying to duplicate his experiments," she replied. "I've already told you too much."

She stood up. "Now, if I were you, I'd put this idea out of your mind and start studying for the Brilliant Brains Trivia Competition. Off you go!"

"But—" Newton protested.

"Off. You. Go," Mumtaz said firmly, with a look that reminded Newton more of a bird of prey than of any tropical songbird.

The four friends left Mumtaz's office.

"Well, that was a dead end," Shelly said. "Don't worry, Newton. We'll find some other way to figure out who your secret relative is."

"Do we have to do it now?" Higgy asked. "I wouldn't mind studying for the trivia contest. That set of encyclopedias is an awesome prize."

Shelly nodded. "Yeah, there are three whole volumes on monsters." Then she frowned. "But we should really help Newton."

"No, go study," Newton urged.

"Come with us!" Theremin said.

"Nah, it's okay," Newton said. "I don't think I'm going to enter the contest anyway. I don't have enough facts in my head to win without using the whole noodle-you-know-what thing. And that feels like cheating."

"It's not cheating!" Theremin argued. "It's part of who you are."

Newton shrugged. "I'm not really sure who I am, Theremin," he said. "See you guys later."

Feeling discouraged, Newton turned and walked away from his friends, outside the school, and back to his dorm room. He climbed to the top bunk and stared at the ceiling.

Mumtaz had said she didn't know anything about his relative, but he wasn't sure if he believed her. She seemed to be connected to everything else that had happened to Newton. But if she wasn't going to help him, how was he going to find his family member?

What had Theremin said about DNA? It determined how you looked. Higgy had said that family members didn't always look alike, but Newton knew that sometimes they did. Shelly looked like a mini version of her mom. Debbie Danning and her twin brother, Donnie Danning, had the same brown hair, the same turned-up noses, and around the same number of freckles.

Newton sat up and grabbed his tablet. He pressed a button, and a hologram of the student and teacher directory appeared in front of him. It had a photo of every student, along with their name and grade, as well as every teacher and the name of the classes they taught.

"Okay, let's see who looks like me," Newton said out loud. "We'll start with the *A*s. Adam Atomico."

The 3-D image of a short, chubby boy with light

brown skin, dark brown eyes, and curly black hair popped up in midair and revolved in front of Newton.

Newton looked down at his tall, thin, pale-skinned body. Nope. And Newton had green eyes, not brown. He did have black hair, but it had a white streak.

Probably not, Newton thought with a sigh. He swiped his tablet, and Amy Azerath replaced Adam Atomico.

Newton frowned. "Red hair, blue eyes. Probably not. . . ."

He scrolled and scrolled, looking for a face that reminded him of his own. Then he felt a tingle on his back that told him someone was coming, and he quickly exited the directory as Higgy oozed into the room.

"What do you say, Newton? Want to eat with us?" Higgy asked.

"Uh, sure," Newton said, sliding down from the bunk.

Higgy paused. "Don't worry, pal. We'll find your family."

"Thanks, Higgy," Newton said, but he was feeling less excited than he had been that morning.

Maybe Mumtaz was right. If Flubitus was confused, all of Newton's hopes were for nothing!

Never Mind

"Today, class, we're going to discuss channeling electricity from lightning," Professor Juvinall announced. "Shelly, as a descendant of Victor Frankenstein, you may already be familiar with this."

"Actually, I'm not," Shelly replied. "My branch of the family broke off from the Frankensteins, so until I did the musical, I didn't know much about him."

"You were great in that, by the way," Professor Juvinall said. "Will you sign my autograph bear?"

"Sure," Shelly said, and she approached the professor's desk, which came up to about Shelly's knees. That's because Professor Juvinall was only six years old.

The professor reached into a drawer and pulled out a canvas bear that she handed to Shelly. "Thanks!"

Shelly signed the bear and walked back to her chair, blushing.

"You're a celebrity, Shelly!" Theremin whispered.

"Now, where were we?" Juvinall asked. "Right. Using the power of lightning!"

"Professor Juvinall, why are we doing this?" Odifin asked, his voice crackling through its speaker. "Harnessing lightning is as old as creating three-legged frogs. We have so many other ways to generate electricity in modern times that are more efficient."

"I'm sorry, Odifin, but are you the professor, or am I?" Professor Juvinall snapped.

"You don't need me to answer that," Odifin snapped back. "I'm just trying to make the point that working with lightning might be a waste of time."

Newton turned to look at Odifin. He was always opinionated, but Newton hadn't seen him challenge a professor before.

Professor Juvinall raised an eyebrow. "Oh, really? Is there something you'd rather be doing with your time than be in this class, Mr. Pinkwad?"

"I can think of a BAZILLION things! Literally!" Odifin responded.

Juvinall pointed to the door. "Fine. Then go do them. Get out of my class."

"With pleasure!" Odifin said. "Come, Rotwang!"

Rotwang stood up and slouched as he walked after Odifin, and they left the room.

Professor Juvinall stuck her tongue out at the departing Odifin, and then turned and glared at her students. "Does anybody else have a complaint about today's lesson?"

Nobody made a peep. Juvinall might have been only six years old, but she had the ability to inspire fear in people ten times her age (and nineteen times her age, if you included Professor Wagg).

"Now, then," Professor Juvinall said. "Please check your tablets to see who you'll be partnered with for today's lesson. Then come up and get some bottled lightning for your group."

Newton looked at his tablet, hoping to see Shelly's or Theremin's name. Instead *Gustav Goddard* came up. Newton looked across the room to see a dark-haired boy with a friendly face motioning for Newton to sit next to him.

Oh well, Newton thought as he sat next to Gustav. *I didn't get Shelly or Theremin, but at least I know Gustav, and he's nice.*

"Thank you, Newton," Gustav said. "I think you're nice too!"

"You're wel— Wait!" Newton said. "Did I say that out loud? Because I thought I was just thinking it."

Gustav grinned. "You *were* thinking it," he replied. He pointed to a device strapped to his wrist that resembled

a watch. "I read your mind. It's a device I've been work-ing on with Maxima van Schmarty."

Newton's eyes widened.

"Newton! Gustav! Come up and get your lightning!" Professor Juvinall called out.

Newton jogged up to the front desk and grabbed a bottle full of sparkling, sizzling miniature lightning.

"Careful with that, Newton," Juvinall said. "It is not a toy."

"Yes, Professor," Newton said, and he slowly walked back to Gustav.

Suddenly he lost his footing! He tripped forward, and almost face-planted. Thanks to his sticky fingers, he didn't lose his grip on the bottle, but he rolled over quickly to avoid smashing it against the floor.

A few of the kids around him clapped, and as Newton got to his feet, he saw Mimi in the seat right next to him, grinning.

"Gosh, Newton, I guess my foot must have gotten in your way," Mimi said, looking down her nose at him.

Why is she so mean to me? Newton wondered. Then he had another thought. *We kind of have the same nose. Maybe she's my sister!*

"Why do you want Mimi, of all people, to be your sister?" Gustav asked as Newton placed the

lightning bottle on the table in front of them.

"You know, it's kind of not cool to read other people's minds, and even less cool to say their thoughts out loud," Newton said.

"Good point," Gustav said. "I won't do it anymore. The watch only works for ten minutes, anyway. Then everything gets garbled until I reset it. Maxima and I are still working out the kinks."

"And the person you use it on doesn't know that you're using it?" Newton asked.

Gustav shook his head. "No, that's the beauty of it. All you have to do is get within a meter of them with the watch." He took an earpiece out of his ear that Newton hadn't noticed before. "And with this earpiece the thoughts are translated into words that you hear inside your ear through a tiny speaker."

"That's amazing!" Newton said.

"Newton! Gustav! Get cracking!" Professor Juvinall snapped.

The boys stopped talking and followed the instructions on their tablet to complete the activity, which involved using wires to channel the electricity from the lightning to make a bell ring. As they worked, an idea formed in Newton's mind.

Flubitus wouldn't tell him who his relative was. But

Flubitus knew. If Newton could read the professor's mind, maybe he could learn what Flubitus didn't want to tell him!

After about twenty minutes, the room was filled with the sound of ringing bells. Newton and Gustav recorded their results, and the room was filled with chatter as students finished up.

"Gustav, can I borrow your mind-reading device?" Newton asked. "I really— It's important."

Gustav frowned. "I don't know. It's still in the prototype stage. And Maxima and I were going to work on it tonight."

"I'll get it back to you before classes are over today," Newton promised.

Gustav nodded. "Okay. Let me know how it works for you."

He unbuckled the device from his wrist and handed it to Newton. Instead of a watch face, the device had a square-shaped screen with swirling blue and purple lights. Gustav took the earpiece out of his ear and handed it to Newton.

"Press the button on the side of the screen to activate it," Gustav instructed. "But there's only about three minutes left before it gets garbled."

"That should be enough," Newton said. "Thanks!"

The bell rang, and Newton ran to find Theremin and Shelly.

"Guys, you won't believe it," Newton said.

"Chances are, I will," Theremin said. "You're a pretty honest guy."

Newton held out his wrist. "This is a mind-reading machine, and I'm going to use it on Professor Flubitus."

"Is that Gustav's?" Shelly asked. "I heard he was working on one."

Newton nodded. "He lent it to me. It's only good for three minutes right now, but that's all I need. I'll ask Flubitus again who my relative is, and even if he won't tell me, the name will pop up in his head."

"That's brilliant, Newton!" Theremin said. "Want us to go with you?"

"We shouldn't," Shelly said. "We don't want Flubitus to be distracted. He gets distracted enough already."

"That makes sense," Newton said. "I'll go see him at lunchtime. Then I'll let you know what I found out."

"It's going to work, Newton," Shelly said, smiling. "You're going to learn who your relative is!"

Newton could barely concentrate through his next classes. When it was time for lunch, he sought out Professor Flubitus.

The green-haired professor was at his desk, eating a

tuna sandwich. Newton could tell it was tuna because it smelled fishy, and because most of it had dribbled down the man's red-and-yellow polka-dot shirt.

"Professor Flubitus," Newton said.

Flubitus looked up. "Newton! How can I help you?"

Newton felt to make sure the earpiece was in place. He casually pressed the button on the side of the mind-reading device. The blue and purple lights swirled on the screen. Newton cleared his throat.

"I really hope you can tell me who my relative at school is," Newton said. "If I have family, I want to know who they are."

"But I told you, Newton, I can't tell you," Flubitus replied. "As it is, I never should have said anything in the first place. There are very serious reasons why . . ."

Newton heard a buzzing in his ear, and then a mechanical voice began to spew out the professor's thoughts. Newton felt his pulse get faster. He was about to get his question answered!

Tuna's dry today. I really need to get a jar of that purple mayonnaise that Professor Phlegm uses; he swears by it.

Newton frowned. How could Flubitus be talking about one thing and be thinking about another? But one random thought after another kept spilling out of Flubitus's mind.

The other day poor Professor Wells asked me if butterflies existed in this dimension. Imagine that! A dimension with no butterflies? How sad.

Come to think of it, I'd love to get a butterfly-patterned vest. Getting tired of these polka dots. Is there even a clothing shop on the island? Or did that shop open up in the future? I can't keep track of what time line I'm in anymore.

That's a nice watch Newton's wearing. The swirling lights are very pretty.

Butterflies are pretty. Poor Wells. I thought being stuck in the past was bad, but I guess being stuck in two dimensions is worse. I'll have to take him out to lunch one of these days. I wonder if he likes tuna.

Newton tried to ask his question again. "Does this mean you're never going to tell me who my relative is? Can't you just give me a clue? Tell me something about them? Anything?"

If I told Newton a clue, he'd be sure to figure it out. He's a smart lad. Thank goodness for that. Do I have any chips in this drawer? Chips and tuna are a great combination.

Wait a second. Is that a watch, or is that the mind-reading device that's all the rage in the future? Are you trying to read my mind, Newton? Because that is—

Skkkkccchhhhh! Skkkkccchhhhh! Grrrrrgggggggggggle!

Skkkkrrrnnnnnch! The device started to glitch.

"See you later, Professor," Newton said quickly, and he ran out of the room and took the winding stairs up to the cafeteria.

He found Theremin, Shelly, and Higgy at their usual table.

"Shelly and Theremin told me about your plan," Higgy said. "Did it work?"

Newton nodded. "The technology worked, but Flubitus's mind was wandering all over the place, and then time ran out. But I'm going to ask Gustav if I can try again."

But as he said the words, Gustav walked up to him.

"Newton, I need my mind reader back," he said. "I just got a message from Mumtaz. She said she got wind of the watch, and mind-reading technology is banned at the school. Something about privacy laws."

Newton cringed. He was pretty sure Flubitus had reported seeing a mind-reading watch, and that was Newton's fault.

"Thanks, Gustav," he said. Then he remembered something Flubitus had said. "But hold on to your research. I have a hunch that you and Maxima will make it happen one day and it's going to be all the rage in the future!"

Gustav grinned. "Thanks, Newton."

Newton sank into his chair and sighed.

"Do you want to share my brussels sprouts casserole?" Higgy asked. "I smothered it in strawberry gelatin."

Newton shook his head. "I'm not hungry."

"Don't lose hope, Newton," Theremin said. "We'll find your family."

"How?" Newton asked. "We can't do DNA tests. Flubitus won't tell me who my relative is. It could be anyone!"

"Well, I've got a theory," Theremin said. "And I don't think it could be just *anyone*. You have memories of being born in a pod. You have no memories of your actual family. And when you asked the portal pass to send you home, you stayed right here. Which maybe means that your true home—is Franken-Sci High."

Newton knew all of this. The portal pass had been a prize for winning the mad science fair. It allowed the school's transportation portal to take you anywhere in the world. But when he'd asked the portal to bring him home, he had stayed put. At first he'd thought there was a glitch. But after Flubitus had arrived, it had seemed like Newton was tied to the school in some important way.

"Maybe there's somebody else here with a story like yours," Theremin continued. "We can be like detectives on a secret mission, and interview other students to find out clues about their history. We can find out a lot with good old-fashioned detective work!"

"Yes!" Shelly cried. "Like, maybe we'll discover some other kid who doesn't know who his or her family is. Or someone who grew up with an egg-like pod in the house."

"We can ask if they come from a place with a lot of amphibians," Higgy teased. "You know, like from a swamp or a pond."

"Very funny," Newton said. "But I like this idea. We can come up with a list of questions." Then he paused. "This will take up a lot of time. Don't you guys need to study for the trivia contest?"

"We can do both," Shelly promised.

"Yes. This is important," Higgy said.

"Plus, I'm doing great at studying," Theremin added. "I really feel like I have a chance this year."

Newton smiled at his friends. "I wish all of you could win."

"As much as I want those encyclopedias, I do think Theremin has a good chance," Higgy said. "Unless . . ."

"Unless what?" Theremin asked.

"Unless Mimi cheats," Shelly said.

"No, I'm not worried about her," Higgy said. "Mimi's smart, but she'll try to cheat, and that never works out for her. But Odifin is taking this whole thing way too seriously. He spends all his time in the library, studying. And today he actually *corrected* Professor Phlegm! And Odifin was right! It's like he's getting smarter."

"No problem. It'll be his soggy brain cells up against my quick-firing circuits," Theremin said confidently. "Odifin Pinkwad doesn't stand a chance of winning the Brilliant Brains Trivia Competition!"

The Latest in Bluegoo Technology

"I told you, there are only two weeks until the competition, Rotwang," Odifin said. "I need to connect to the brains in the Brain Bank every spare minute!"

"But you woke me up at five o'clock this morning, and I'm tired," Rotwang complained.

"I don't see why you're tired," Odifin replied. "I'm the one doing all the studying. All you do is play with those virtual reality goggles of yours. Which is annoying, because sometimes when I need you, I can't rouse you from whatever silly thing you're doing."

"I go to the virtual zoo," Rotwang said. "I like the virtual reptile house."

"Well, do it on your own time!" Odifin snapped.

"I don't have *any* time of my own," Rotwang replied. "We're always in the Brain Bank! And according to the Mad Scientist–Assistant Treaty of 1897, I'm supposed to get one hour of free time every day."

"You're also supposed to call me 'Master,'" Odifin shot back. "But you don't always do that, do you?"

Rotwang scowled. "No."

"No, what?" Odifin said.

"No . . . Master," Rotwang replied.

"Now let's get going," Odifin said. "I want to try to download information from at least two brains tonight. At this rate I'll never get enough information to win the contest!"

"You've already downloaded information from, like, twenty brains," Rotwang remarked. "Isn't that enough? It almost looks like you're getting bigger."

"That's exactly what I *need* to happen," Odifin said. "The bigger I am, the more knowledge I can hold! But I wouldn't expect your puny brain to comprehend that."

He rolled away, and Rotwang followed him. It was after dinner, and only a few of the most studious students were in the library. The Brain Bank was deserted, except for Odifin, Rotwang, and the brains. Odifin made quick progress. Rotwang hooked Odifin up to one brain and then another, and eventually Odifin was ready to connect to a third brain. It was the brain of Selena Luciano, who had perfected a method of communicating with plants.

Odifin was eager to download all of Selena Luciano's

knowledge as quickly as possible.

Ciao! Selena said. *It's the boy on wheels! How nice. I've been hoping you'd stop by for a chat.*

Since this was his third brain in a row, he'd stopped with any pleasantries.

"Just a simple download, please," Odifin said. "Neuron to neuron."

Mamma mia, you're just like every other student in this school, Selena complained. *Nobody ever wants to chat.*

"Download. Please," Odifin said, emotionless.

Then he settled in as the data flowed into his brain. He could feel the tingle as his nerve endings sparked. He wondered if what Rotwang had said was true—that he was getting bigger. He didn't often look into a mirror. But the thought of getting bigger felt right. Why not? Didn't other kids his age get taller, or wider? Why couldn't he? After all, the brain is kind of like a muscle, and when you use muscles, they get stronger—and bigger.

The download from Selena took several hours, and when she'd finished, she started chatting again.

Now that we're done, maybe you could tell me a little bit about the world outside this room? she asked. *Right before I died, they invented gelato. . . . That's ice cream. Do they still have ice cream?*

"Rotwang! Detach me!" Odifin yelled.

Rotwang, as usual, was wearing his virtual reality goggles. He slipped them up onto the top of his head.

"One second," he said. "I need to plug my goggles in to recharge."

"Rotwang, unplug me right now!" Odifin demanded, as Selena droned on and on about ice cream. Helpless, Odifin watched as his assistant searched the walls for an outlet.

"Look to your right, you dolt! There's a control panel there!" Odifin said.

Rotwang moved to the control panel. "There's no outlet here," he said. "Just a lot of brain names. And a port that says *Select All*."

"Wait, what?" Odifin asked. "Say that again."

Rotwang nodded. "There's no outlet here," he repeated.

"No, about that other thing you said," Odifin hinted.

"Just a lot of brain names?" Rotwang tried.

"No, the *other* other thing!" Odifin shouted.

"Oh, the port that says *Select All*?" Rotwang asked.

"Yes!" Odifin said. "Has that port been there all along?" Odifin asked.

Rotwang shrugged.

"Don't just stand there! Connect me to it!" Odifin demanded.

Rotwang obeyed, detaching Odifin from Selena's jar,

holding the connector as they went over to the control panel, and then plugging the connector into the *Select All* port.

Immediately Odifin's brain began to tingle and sizzle and hum more than it ever had before, as the data from every brain in the Brain Bank poured into his cells.

"This is awesome, Rotwang!" Odifin yelled over the noise that only he could hear.

Rotwang nodded and went off to search for a plug to charge his goggles.

For hours information flowed, filling Odifin with facts and figures, names and places, dates and times, formulas and equations. For someone else it might have been too much to handle, but it only made Odifin thirsty for more knowledge.

"More, more, more!" Odifin cried out, even though all he had to do to get more information was stay plugged in.

Eventually, though, Odifin began to notice an unpleasant sensation. Brains don't have pain receptors, but he felt pressure—as if his membranes were pressing against the walls and top of his jar.

"Rotwang, what's happening?" Odifin asked.

There was no response. His eyeball stalks twisted around to see Rotwang, asleep and snoring on the floor, with his virtual reality glasses still on.

"ROTWANG!" Odifin yelled.

Rotwang jumped, and his glasses slid off. Then his eyes got wide.

"Master, you're HUGE!" he said. "You're busting out of your jar!"

"Excellent!" Odifin said. "Rotwang, get me out of this tiny jar!"

"But won't you die?" Rotwang gulped.

"No," Odifin replied. "Mother put me inside this jar to keep me from getting squashed, or dusty, or bruised. The fluid keeps me from drying out, of course, but I don't need this jar. It's just a silly safety measure. Get me out, now!"

Rotwang glanced at the speaker box on the jar. "What about talking?"

"Do I have to explain everything?" Odifin asked. "We use the animation fluid to connect me to the data panel on my jar, which acts like a voice box and connects to the speaker I use to talk and to the port that lets me connect to the Brain Bank."

Rotwang stared at him blankly.

"The animation fluid is the goo! The goo in my jar!" Odifin yelled, exasperated. "Now roll that metal cart over here and detach the jar from the table. Then GET ME OUT OF HERE!"

Rotwang unscrewed the jar from the table, removed the lid, and then turned the jar upside down and shook it.

"Gently, Rotwang, gently! And over the cart, please! I don't want to end up on the floor. It's covered with germs!" Odifin cried. "And don't forget to put my

original jar on the cart too. I need it."

Rotwang held the jar in one hand and pulled the cart over with the other. He turned the jar upside down again and shook it.

With a slimy, slurping sound Odifin slid free from the jar and onto the cart, dripping with goo. Rotwang quickly put the jar on the cart too. The goo splashed all over the top of the cart but was still touching the jar's data panel and port, which was still plugged into the room's control panel through the connector.

Odifin felt the same and yet so, so different. He gazed around the room. How clear the world looked when he wasn't gazing through a jar full of goo! He stretched his eyestalks to get a better look at Rotwang.

"Wow, Rotwang. I didn't know you had so many pimples!" Odifin exclaimed.

"Uh, thanks?" Rotwang replied, sounding surprised but also proud.

All the while, facts and figures, names and places, dates and times, formulas and equations continued to flow into Odifin's memory banks.

"Rotwang, disconnect me from the control panel for a minute," he said, and his assistant obeyed.

Suddenly it was quiet for Odifin. "Now I can really think," he said. His synapses sizzled as an idea formed

in his head. "As good as it feels to be out of the jar, Mother was right. I will dry up without my goo—I mean, animation fluid," he told Rotwang. "We will need to borrow a big fish tank from the monster lab for me to use. Of course, it won't have a speaker, or a port, but that won't be a problem. We can attach my old jar to the tank since it acts like my voice box. Then I can find a way to wirelessly connect to the Brain Bank so I don't need a port. Plus I'll need bigger speakers, and they'll need to be wireless too. Rotwang, you use wireless speakers with your video game system, right?"

"Uh-huh," Rotwang replied.

"I'll need those," Odifin said.

Rotwang frowned. "But—"

"And we'll need some nanobots," Odifin went on. "So you'll have to sneak into the robotics lab for me."

"But—"

"NOW, Rotwang!"

With a burst of speed, Rotwang pushed the cart, with Odifin on it, out of the Brain Bank. The hallways of the school were dark, and there was no sign of Stubbins Crouch, the custodian. First Odifin and Rotwang went to the monster lab to get the fish tank. Tiny monsters snored in locked cages, but the equipment closet wasn't locked, and Odifin spotted an

empty aquarium tank that was the perfect size.

"Put it on the cart, Rotwang," Odifin instructed.

Rotwang rolled Odifin—and the cart and fish tank—to the next destination: Dr. Rozika's robotics lab. Odifin scanned the room and spotted a locked vault.

"He keeps the nanobots in there," Odifin said.

Rotwang tried to open it. "It's locked."

"Roll me closer," Odifin told him, and Rotwang did. "It's a retinal scanner," Odifin said. "Only Dr. Rozika can open it. Unless . . ."

Odifin's brain sizzled with all the knowledge he'd accumulated. "Rotwang, open up the panel on the side of the vault. We can bypass the retinal scan with some simple coding. Do as I say . . ."

Rotwang followed Odifin's instructions exactly, and the vault opened. Rotwang removed a small metal box containing the nanobots.

"Next we need your speakers!" Odifin said. "And then we can put all of this together in the chemistry lab."

Rotwang yawned. "It's so late!"

"No time to sleep, Rotwang!" Odifin yelled. "Anyway, I know you stay up all night playing video games sometimes, so what are you complaining about?"

Odifin had never felt so confident before. Or so smart. And that made him feel alive! More alive than

he'd ever felt in his whole life.

He barked out orders to Rotwang so fast that the boy could barely follow them.

"First we program the nanobots to act as wireless conductors," he said. "Then we add them to the goo to make super goo that's able to connect wirelessly to your wireless speakers and anything else with wireless capabilities. We'll attach your wireless speakers to the tank and keep everything on the metal cart so that you can wheel me around. We'll have to figure out a way to motorize it, but . . . No. Instead we can create a wireless receiver that you can plug into the control panel in the Brain Bank. Then I can wirelessly download data from the Brain Bank day and night from wherever I am!"

"What about class?" Rotwang asked.

"Nobody will miss me," Odifin said. "Nobody ever notices me anyway. But they will, once I win the Brilliant Brains Trivia Competition!"

They worked through the night, and when the sun rose, Odifin was floating inside the fish tank, inside super goo that Rotwang had made with Odifin's instructions. The chemicals added to keep the nanobots charged had added streaks of glowing blue to the goo, which reminded Odifin of lightning.

"This is brilliant!" Odifin said. "I feel truly amazing,

Rotwang! Rotwang? Rotwang!"

His assistant was snoring again.

"Wake up, you lazy bones!" Odifin scolded.

At that moment Professor Snollygoster swept into the lab in his white lab coat.

"Good morning, boys," he said. "You're a bit early for class, aren't you?"

"Just doing some extra studying, Professor," Odifin replied.

"Odifin, is there something different about you?" Snollygoster asked. "You look . . . bigger. And is that new goo?"

"Yes," Odifin replied. "I call it . . . super bluegoo!"

"Has a nice ring to it," Snollygoster said.

"Yes, it does," Odifin said. "Rotwang, let's go!"

They exited the chemistry lab.

"Where are we going now?" Rotwang asked.

"Back to the Brain Bank," Odifin said.

Rotwang grumbled but he did as he was told. Odifin floated in the super bluegoo as Rotwang pushed the metal cart back to the library. Then Rotwang plugged the wireless-capable super bluegoo receiver into the *Select All* port.

Odifin felt his neurons bursting with tingles. "It's working!" he said. "I estimate that the receiver has a

range of about four-point-eight meters, so we'll have to stay here in the Brain Bank for now, Rotwang. If anyone tries to come in, tell them to get lost."

Rotwang yawned. "Yes, Master," he said, and then he curled up on the floor and began to snore.

The information flooded into Odifin again: facts and figures, names and places, dates and times, formulas and equations. His membranes started to pulse.

Excellent! he thought. *I won't stop until my memory banks contain every iota of knowledge in Franken-Sci High!*

And as he absorbed that knowledge, his brain slowly began to grow even bigger. . . .

CHAPTER 6

An Overgrown Ball of Glop

"So, Debbie, how's it going?" Newton asked, sliding onto a stool next to Debbie Danning in the chemistry lab.

"Fine," Debbie said. "What's up?"

"Oh, you know. I realized that with my amnesia and everything, I don't know a lot about the other kids in the school," Newton said, trying to sound casual and friendly. "You and Donnie, where are you guys from?"

"Seattle, Washington," Debbie replied, and Newton stared at her blankly. "In the United States."

"Right! I've heard of those," Newton said. "And you guys were born in a regular hospital, right?"

Debbie made a face. "What kind of question is that?"

"Just a very normal, friendly question," Newton replied. "I mean, being born is a pretty important thing, right?"

"I guess," Debbie said. "But we weren't born in a hospital."

A flame of hope rose in Newton. "No?"

"Well, Dad was all nervous, and when he tried to teleport Mom to the hospital, we ended up in the rain forest of Borneo," Debbie explained. "Mom is still mad about that. But luckily, Donnie and I came out okay." Debbie pressed a button on her tablet, and a screen flickered in midair.

"That's me and Donnie right after we were born. I was born five minutes earlier, so I'm older," she explained.

"Right," Newton said. The screen showed a woman holding two babies wrapped in leaves near a giant flower, but there was no sign of a pod. Newton tried another line of questioning.

"So, are you a good swimmer? Like, so good that you can breathe underwater?" he asked.

Debbie rolled her eyes. "Listen, Newton, if you want to ask me out, just ask me. You don't have to lead with a bunch of silly questions."

"Ask you out?" Newton started to blush. "No. I mean, sure, that would be . . . but—that's not what I—bye!"

He hurried away and sat next to Theremin.

"How did it go?" Theremin asked.

"She thought I was asking her out," Newton said.

"So you didn't find out anything?" Theremin asked.

"Well, I learned that she and Donnie were born in a rain forest," Newton said.

Theremin tapped his tablet screen. "Hmm. That makes six students born in some kind of forest, three on a space station, and two in an alternate universe."

"Any pods yet?" Newton asked.

"Nope," Theremin replied. "And no cases of amnesia, or long-lost relatives, or amphibious traits, like you have."

Newton sighed. "This isn't working, Theremin. I think we've talked to almost everyone in the school at this point."

"'Almost' doesn't mean this is over," Theremin said.

"No," Newton said. "I just wish Professor Flubitus would tell me. Or Mumtaz! I know she knows something. If she hadn't confiscated Gustav's mind-reading device, I'd try it on her."

Newton slumped in his seat.

"Maybe you don't have to read her mind," Theremin said. "She's got files on every student, right?"

"Shelly and I tried sneaking into Mumtaz's office once before," Newton said. "That's the first time I camouflaged. I didn't even realize I had done it."

"Oh yeah," Theremin said. "That was before you got better at it."

"I did get better at it, didn't I?" Newton said. "I can control it more now. I could camouflage myself and sneak into her office again, and this time it might work!"

"I'll go with you," Theremin said. "Or Shelly or

Higgy will. You shouldn't do this alone."

Newton shook his head. "No, you guys have done enough. I don't want you to get in trouble. Besides, I thought Shelly had set up a study session for you guys at the library tonight."

"Yeah, well, we were going to go to the Brain Bank, but Gustav told me that something weird is going on there. Rotwang won't let anyone in," Theremin said.

"Rotwang?" Newton asked.

Theremin nodded. "Yeah. Probably Odifin wants to hog all the brains for himself. Typical. So Shelly's doing this thing where she's looking up questions from the last few trivia contests, and we're going to test ourselves. Are you sure you don't want to come?"

Newton shook his head. "I really want to figure out who my relative is."

"Sure, Newton," Theremin said. "But just remember, no matter what happens, I'll always be your robot bro."

"Ro-bro," Newton said, combining the words "robot" and "bro" for fun, and he smiled for the first time all day.

"Yeah. Ro-bro," Theremin said. "I like it!"

That night, after the sun had gone down and the school was quiet, Newton dropped down through Higgy's secret entrance to the school's underground tunnels. Higgy had a trapdoor hidden under his bunk bed that he used in order to go on midnight snack runs to the cafeteria (among other things). Newton walked in a tunnel until he spotted the grate leading to Mumtaz's office above him, and stopped. He tried to sense if there was anyone in the room. He didn't feel that tingly feeling he got when there was danger, so he pushed up the grate, pulled himself up, and went inside.

No one was there, so he stood up and quietly replaced the grate. He moved toward Mumtaz's desk, where she accessed the school database using a hologram. He waved his hand in the air, and a hologram of the database appeared.

"Yes!" Newton cheered in a whisper. Then he stopped. *What if someone walks in?* he thought. He knew what he had to do. *Camouflage,* he told himself, and he closed his eyes, concentrating. When he opened them, he saw that his body was shadowy gray, and patterned with the shelves and objects on the wall behind him.

Now stay! he thought. He hadn't had too much practice with camouflaging himself on command, but he knew he could keep it going as long as he kept

thinking about it, especially if he was scared.

Newton looked back at the hologram. He took his ID and swiped it through the hologram projector. That's what Mumtaz had done to call up his file on his very first day.

ENTER PASSWORD

"Rats!" Newton said. "I should have known there would be a password."

He thought for a minute. Then he typed in *Mumtaz*.

INCORRECT

He tried again. *Birdlady*.

INCORRECT

He was about to take a guess when he felt a tingle.

Mumtaz is coming! he thought. Still camouflaged, he waved his hand in the air again to get rid of the database. Then he took a step away from the desk as the doorknob turned, and Mumtaz entered the room. Newton tried not to breathe, and his heart was pounding.

The headmistress was talking on her wireless headset.

"I know you're here to protect him, Professor Flubitus, but I really think you need to keep away from him," Mumtaz was saying. "You can't keep yourself from talking. You almost gave away some very important information!"

Newton's heart pounded faster. Were Mumtaz and

Professor Flubitus talking about him?

"I know the boy deserves to know, but just think of what kind of a quantum quagmire that would open," Mumtaz said. "If he knew that his brother was a . . ."

Mumtaz stopped, and Newton had to keep himself from screaming.

Was a what? he wanted to yell. And also, *I have a brother!*

But Mumtaz didn't finish. Her attention snapped to the video monitors for the library security cameras. "Professor, I've got to go," she said, and then she hurried out of the office.

Still camouflaged, Newton followed her. He wasn't sure why. But he was spurred on by the hope that Mumtaz would say, or mutter out loud, the name of his brother. He raced behind Mumtaz as she hurried to the library. At one point she stopped, turned, and looked behind her. Newton froze. Her eyes narrowed, but she turned back and continued on.

She didn't stop until she got to the Brain Bank. When she walked in, she gasped.

"Oh my goodness, Odifin!"

Newton carefully stepped forward and saw that all the brain jars had been pushed against the wall to make room for a blue plastic kiddie pool in the center of the

room. Inside the kiddie pool was a huge brain with eyes—a brain that looked very much like Odifin, but way bigger, about the size of a teacher's desk. Rotwang was wearing a wet suit and using a plastic beach pail to pour blue goop over Odifin.

"More super bluegoo, Rotwang! I'm starting to dry out!" Odifin said.

"Odifin, what is the meaning of this?" Mumtaz asked.

"KNOWLEDGE!" Odifin's reply thundered through the wireless speakers. "I am absorbing more knowledge than any student has ever absorbed before! That is what's going on."

Mumtaz pursed her lips together. "I see," she said. "I certainly am in favor of knowledge, Odifin, but if you get any bigger, you're going to knock over all these jars."

"Don't you think I know that?" Odifin snapped, and Mumtaz raised an eyebrow. "Tori Twitcher has agreed to lend me the tank she used to display her mechanical shark, which should be big enough, and Rotwang has been building me a new platform using the printer in the 3-D lab. It should be ready momentarily. I've increased the range of my super bluegoo receiver, and Rotwang has created another batch of goo for me. I was planning on moving into my new dwelling tonight.

Unfortunately, my dorm room is not big enough to hold me either."

"There is plenty of room in the basement," Mumtaz said. "Rotwang, go fetch the platform and the tank."

Then she reached into the front pocket of her jacket and pulled out a fly drone. "Find Tori Twitcher and tell her that Rotwang is coming for the shark tank."

The drone flew off. By this point students who'd been studying in the library had all gathered at the entrance to the Brain Bank and were staring at Odifin. Newton stepped aside and stopped camouflaging. There was no need for that now.

He found Shelly, Theremin, and Higgy.

"Hey, Newton," Shelly said. "So it looks like Odifin's been growing, huh?"

Newton nodded. "Yeah," he said. "Is that supposed to happen?"

"Why not?" Theremin asked. "Before you came to the school, André Wadlow invented a growth formula and sprouted up to nine feet tall! He doesn't go to the school anymore, though."

Newton looked up. "Because the ceilings aren't high enough?"

"No, because he couldn't find any pants that fit," Theremin replied.

"Weird events happen all the time at Franken-Sci High," Higgy added. "Last year the entire mad-science-fiction book club became miniaturized for twenty-four hours! Everyone thought they were missing, but the cafeteria ladies found them diving into the nacho dip."

Shelly lowered her voice. "I thought you were sneaking into Mumtaz's office tonight," she whispered.

"I did," he answered. "I couldn't get into the database, but I heard Mumtaz talking to Flubitus. And she said I have a *brother*."

Shelly's eyes got wide. "That's great! It narrows down our search."

"I hope it's me," Theremin said. "I mean, it's not impossible, right? Maybe my dad had something to do with creating you, too."

"You never know," Newton said, and he felt more excited than he'd felt in a long time. He was getting closer to finding out who his relative was!

At that moment, Rotwang appeared holding a remote control that was guiding a large motorized platform topped with a huge glass tank. Inside the tank, glowing super bluegoo sloshed around.

"That's the shark tank Tori used at the science fair," Shelly remarked.

The platform wouldn't fit inside the Brain Bank, and Rotwang stopped. He moved over to the kiddie pool and tried to pick it up. But his skinny arms could barely lift it.

"Drones, help him!" Mumtaz called out, and the library drones zoomed into the Brain Bank. Mechanical arms extended from each one, and together they lifted up the kiddie pool. They flew over to the shark tank and tipped it over, and Odifin sloshed into the super bluegoo.

His voice came out of a speaker on the side of the tank. "Ah, much better!"

"Get him down to the boiler room, Rotwang," Mumtaz ordered. "Odifin, we're going to figure out a way for you to attend classes remotely from now on."

"But, Headmistress, I need to—"

"You can attend class, even if it's virtually," Mumtaz said. "You too, Rotwang. No more guarding the Brain Bank for your friend, as I've heard. You're a student at this school too, not just Odifin's assistant."

"Yes, Ms. Mumtaz," Rotwang said, and Newton thought he saw a look of relief on the boy's face.

Rotwang pressed a button on the remote, and the platform began to move out of the library.

"Take the service elevator!" Mumtaz called out.

"You'll see!" Odifin cried as his tank moved past the crowd of onlookers. "Just wait until the Brilliant Brains Trivia Competition! I will defeat you ALL!"

Theremin's eyes flashed. "Is Mumtaz really going to let that overgrown ball of glop compete?" he asked. "That's not fair."

"I don't think there are any rules limiting brain size," Higgy pointed out.

"Well, maybe there should be," Theremin said.

"Just because Odifin is big doesn't mean he's smart," Newton pointed out. "I think you'll do great, ro-bro."

Shelly grinned. "Is this a new thing? It's cute."

Newton nodded.

"Anyway, should we keep studying?" Higgy asked.

"I've got a better idea," Shelly said. "Let's take this new information we've gotten from Newton and try to narrow down our data to find his brother."

"What do you say, Newton?" Higgy asked.

Newton grinned. "Yes!"

CHAPTER 7

One Big, Bored Brain

Soon after, Odifin was on the move. He liked getting so much attention as he traveled through the halls on the giant motorized platform. The halls were just wide enough for the shark tank and platform to fit. Kids stared, wide-eyed, at him as they got out of the platform's way. They pointed and whispered to one another. He even heard one kid yell, "Looking good, Odifin!"

Then Odifin and Rotwang boarded the service elevator to the basement. Odifin rolled out into the dark, damp space, lit by flickering fluorescent lights that cast a sickly glow everywhere. It was quite a change from the bright, colorful library.

"I should speak to Ms. Mumtaz about better quarters," Odifin remarked. "Unless she has a luxury suite set up for me down here."

"She said the boiler room," Rotwang said, and he steered Odifin's tank into a huge space next to the

chugging boilers that heated the school's water tanks.

"I suppose this will have to do," Odifin said. "But it doesn't really matter where I am, Rotwang! With my new advances to the super bluegoo, I can connect to anything in the school just by thinking about it! Every database! Every camera! Every bit of knowledge in the school is now mine."

"Cool," Rotwang said, unimpressed. "So, listen, um, Master, since you don't need me to guard the Brain Bank anymore, I should start going to class again, like Ms. Mumtaz said. Unless, you know, you need me to hang out with you?"

"It's not like you're very good company, always wearing those virtual reality glasses," Odifin replied. "Do whatever you want."

"Okay, then. So, good night," Rotwang said, shrugging.

"Is it nighttime?" Odifin asked. "The hours just fly by these days. And I don't seem to need as much rest as I used to. Maybe you could stay for a little longer, Rotwang, and we'll— Rotwang?"

His assistant was gone.

"Fine," Odifin said out loud, to nobody besides himself. "I'll just enhance my intelligence some more until I feel sleepy."

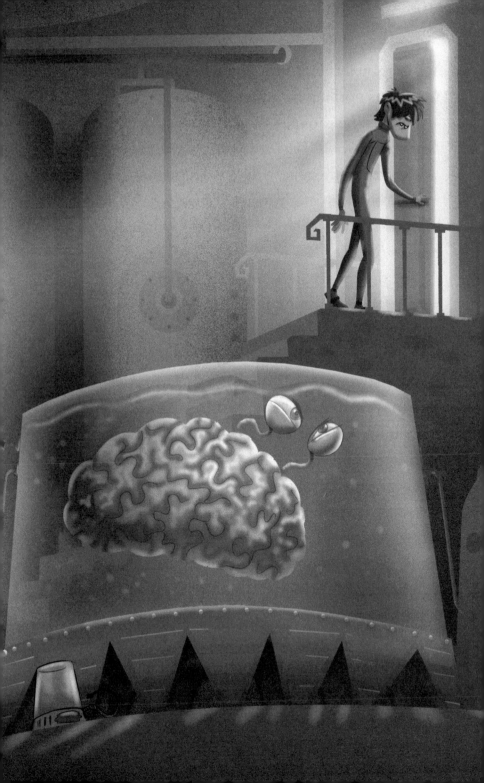

He thought about the brains in the Brain Bank, but there was nothing new there to learn.

Hmmm, he thought. *Where else might the trivia questions come from? The professors, maybe?*

He reached out with his thoughts and tapped into Professor Snollygoster's files for his Emotional Chemistry class. The first file that reached him was a homework file.

"Is this what I've been missing? Equations so simple that a baby could solve them? Ha!" Odifin cried. He solved the problems and shut the file. Then he dug deeper, absorbing all of Snollygoster's notes, tests, and quizzes. "Marvelous," Odifin said. "I can feel myself growing bigger once again. Soon I will have more knowledge than anyone else at Franken-Sci High. And maybe the world! Mwah-ha-ha!"

There was no one to hear his mad-scientist cackle. The only one who might have heard it was the custodian, Stubbins Crouch, who was sweeping the floor in the hallway outside the boiler room, but he didn't hear anything because he had his headphones on. He liked listening to podcasts before heading to his room to sleep.

Odifin actually needed rest too, just like any other brain, and he drifted off to sleep. He dreamed that he

snuck into the tablets of students at school and completed all of their homework assignments. There was something so satisfying about it, getting the answers right one after the other.

When he woke up, he was pulsing with energy.

"What next?" he wondered out loud. "Ah yes, the professors' files."

With his super brainpower it only took him a day to download the course files of every professor, and his brain grew even bigger. He was so preoccupied that he didn't notice when his brain sprouted tendrils that waved in the air like seaweed in water. It was like his main brain couldn't grow any bigger, so it started to sprout and grow branches.

That night he dreamed of completing homework assignments again—hundreds of math problems . . . seventeen chemical formulas. . . . He even wrote a three-thousand-word essay titled "Why Sometimes Being Unethical Is the Ethical Thing to Do" and submitted it as extra credit to Professor Wagg's History of Mad Scientists class for a student named Archimedes Jones, who was failing the class.

"What an unusual dream," Odifin thought when he woke up. "Rotwang, you wouldn't believe what—"

He stopped. *What had Rotwang said? Something*

about going to classes? Odifin wondered.

What a lousy excuse to not have to hang around with me, Odifin thought. Then he spoke out loud.

"Let's see, what shall I do today?" Odifin wondered. "I've downloaded everything the professors know. Maybe it's time to see what Ms. Mumtaz has in her files."

He spent hours trying to break into the headmistress's encrypted files, but not even his overdeveloped brain cells could crack her security. He finally gave up.

"What a waste of time, when I could be learning something," he said. "What else is out there?"

He began to scan everything he could reach with the super bluegoo, and his mind connected to a security drone.

This could be fun, Odifin thought. *To the cafeteria!*

Controlling the drone with his mind, he sent the drone flying through the hallways.

"Sound," Odifin commanded, and then he could hear everything going on around the drone as students walked to the cafeteria.

". . . so weird!" one boy was saying. "I woke up and my homework for Leviathan's class was finished, but I don't remember doing it."

"I got extra credit for something I didn't do!" said Archimedes. "I tried to tell Professor Wagg that it was some kind of mistake, but he didn't believe me."

"Maybe you did it in your sleep," his friend joked.

In your sleep? Odifin thought. Then he had a terrifying and amazing thought. *Maybe those dreams weren't dreams,* Odifin realized. *I must have done all that work I dreamed about when I thought I was sleeping. My brain is so powerful that I can't turn it off!*

The drone entered the cafeteria, and Odifin moved it around. Gustav Goddard was getting a smoothie out of the machine. Odifin connected to the smoothie maker.

Blend faster, Odifin instructed the machine with his thoughts, and the smoothie maker shot green liquid out so quickly that it splattered all over Gustav.

"Hey!" Gustav wailed. "What's wrong with this thing?"

"That was pretty funny," Odifin said out loud in the boiler room. "What next?"

The drone reached Mimi Crowninshield and some other students, and Odifin hovered there, listening.

"I'm telling you, he was big!" Tori Twitcher was saying.

"Bigger than a . . . neo-proton collector?" Mimi asked.

"Yes," Tori said. "Odifin was as big as . . . Mumtaz's hovercraft, I swear! He must be, like, super-intelligent."

Mimi sniffed. "Odifin?"

For fun Odifin made the cafeteria lights flicker when she said his name.

"Odifin"—the lights flickered—"can get as big as he wants, but he will never be as smart as I am," Mimi said. "And if Odifin"—the lights flickered again—"is so smart, where is he now? Why isn't he in class with the rest of us, showing us how smart he is?"

"I don't think he could fit into class," Tori remarked.

Mimi's remarks didn't bother Odifin. He knew he was smarter than anybody else in Franken-Sci High. He was probably the smartest boy in the whole world!

The drone zipped around the cafeteria, and Odifin listened in on the students' conversations. He made the lights flicker every time he heard his name.

Higgy said to Newton, "I heard that Odifin"—the

lights flickered, and Higgy paused. "Hey, did you see that? Did the lights flicker when I said 'Odifin'?" Before Newton could answer, the lights flickered again.

"They did!" Newton said, once the flickering was over. "That's weird."

Odifin was having fun until the drone spotted Rotwang, eating a burger and sitting at a table with two boys that Odifin didn't recognize.

"And then the duck started to cluck like a chicken!" one of the boys was saying, and Rotwang started laughing.

"That's great. You are too funny, Milton," Rotwang said.

An emotion surged through Odifin, a mix of annoyance, anger, and jealousy. The lights flickered off and on, causing all of the kids to quiet down.

"What's happening?" Rotwang wondered aloud.

"Must be a problem with the mainframe," Milton replied.

Odifin broke his connection with the drone, and it crashed to the floor of the cafeteria with a clatter. He reached out to other parts of the school, looking for more things to do. He found Stubbins Crouch in a hallway, steering a robotic floor polisher to clean the yellow-and-green linoleum.

Let's play tag! Odifin thought, and he watched gleefully as the floor polisher chased the poor custodian around and around in circles.

Odifin spent the next few hours finding things to mess with. He broke the codes to every locker and slammed them open and shut, open and shut. He made a lawn mower chew up Professor Lilydale's garden of flowers outside the carnivorous plants lab. He activated a fire-safety sprinkler, drenching a hallway full of kids on their way to class.

He was about to set all the washing machines in the school laundry spinning at a hundred miles per hour when Rotwang appeared. Rotwang took a quick look at Odifin's new brain tendrils and shrugged.

"Oh, hello, Rotwang," Odifin said. "I guess you got bored hanging out with all those unintelligent lunkheads who call themselves mad scientists, and decided to be with me. Smart move. I've been having some fun with—"

Rotwang held out a cell phone. "Your mom's on the phone."

"Odie? Are you okay? You haven't called in ages. And Ms. Mumtaz left me messages about you taking over the Brain Bank and growing?" She sounded worried.

"I'm fine, Mom," Odifin said. "Better than ever, in

fact! Ever since I got settled down here in the basement boiler room, I—"

"Boiler room?" Ms. Pinkwad interrupted. "What on earth are you doing there?"

"I became enhanced by the knowledge I absorbed from the Brain Bank, and as a result I've grown a bit larger," Odifin explained. "But it's fine. I know more about everything than anybody else in the whole school!"

"You mean you aren't going to class?" she asked.

"Didn't you hear me? I already know everything," Odifin replied, and Rotwang, still holding the phone, cringed at Odifin's disrespectful tone. "What do I need with class?"

"Now, don't take that tone with me, Odifin," his mom said. "You know I sent you to Franken-Sci High to make friends and meet people. How can you do that in a basement?"

"I don't need friends, Mom," Odifin replied. "I never have."

"But you told me you had made a lot of friends, Odifin," his mom said.

"I lied," Odifin said.

His mom gasped and said, "You lied?"

"Yes, so you would stop bugging me. I don't have any friends!"

"That's not true. You have Rotwang. He's your friend," his mom said.

"HE IS NOT MY FRIEND!" Odifin shouted. "HE ONLY HANGS OUT WITH ME BECAUSE HE HAS TO! AND HE DOESN'T EVEN HANG OUT WITH ME ANYMORE!"

Behind his mop of hair, Rotwang looked hurt. But he didn't say anything.

"We will talk about this more some other time, Odifin," his mom said. "You need to take ten deep breaths and calm down, young man. Rotwang, if you're still there, I am sorry you had to hear that."

She ended the call. Rotwang gazed up at Odifin.

"Master, I—"

"JUST GO AWAY AND LEAVE ME ALONE!"

Rotwang slunk away without another word.

At first Odifin felt shame. He'd never spoken to his mom like that before. And what he'd said about Rotwang—well, he wasn't sure if it was true. Then he changed his mind. *Of course it's true!* he told himself. *Rotwang deserted you! You don't have any friends, and you never will! Luckily for you, it means that you have nothing to lose.*

Odifin stretched his mind to reach every mechanical device in the school. *Now let's see. What can I do next?*

CHAPTER 8

The Monster in the Basement

"Are we any closer to finding my brother yet?" Newton asked. "It's been two days."

Once they'd found out that Newton had a brother, Theremin had cataloged everyone in the boys' dorm and created a master data bank. He'd deleted everyone they had ruled out, after interviewing them had made it clear they weren't likely to be Newton's brother. That had left them with twenty-three boys still to interview. The friends had split up the list and been interviewing possible brothers whenever they could.

Newton, Theremin, Higgy, and Shelly had decided to compare results at the 3-D Snack Shop after school. It was one of the places located just off campus. The snack shop employed a 3-D printer to make snacks, but used edible building material instead of plastic. Customers could create a snack on the screen by combining flavors (fruity, chocolatey, cheesy, or spicy ones, and many

more) with shapes to make custom creations.

Higgy gobbled down a cheesy-chocolate race car. "I interviewed the seven boys on my list," he said. "None of them fit the profile."

"And I talked to Aristotle Gardyloo, Harold Gubbins, and Tobias Wallamoon," Shelly said, nibbling on a fruity snack shaped like a toad. "They're not good candidates either."

Newton looked at the list he was keeping on his tablet. "And I talked to thirteen more, and it doesn't look like any of them could be my brother either." He sighed. He'd made a fruity-cheesy-spicy spaceship, but he suddenly wasn't hungry at all.

"That's twenty-three!" Theremin gasped. "We've ruled out every boy in the dorms. There are no other boys in the school."

"Unless it's one of the teachers," Shelly suggested. "It could be an older brother."

"In the case of Professor Wagg, that would be an extremely older brother," Higgy joked.

"I can create a new database of teachers," Theremin offered.

"I guess," Newton replied. "But don't worry about doing it now. I know you guys want to study for the trivia competition."

Higgy nodded to Newton's spaceship. "If you're not going to eat that . . ."

"Be my guest," Newton said, and Higgy reached out and swallowed the snack in one gulp.

The friends left the snack shop and walked back to the main school building. As they walked in, Tabitha Talos approached them.

"Hey, have you guys heard the rumor about Odifin Pinkwad?" she asked, and as she did, the overhead lights flickered.

"You mean that he got really big?" Newton asked. "Yeah, we saw it ourselves, a couple of days ago."

"They put Odifin," Shelly began, and the lights flickered again, "in a big, glass shark tank."

"Hey, is anyone else noticing that the lights flicker every time someone says Odifin's name?" Theremin asked. *(Flicker!)*

"Yeah," Higgy said.

"It happened in the cafeteria, too," Shelly added.

"I'm getting creeped out," said Tabitha.

"Odifin?" Newton whispered, and the lights flickered. Then Newton realized something. "Odifin!" he shouted, and the lights flickered again. "We didn't interview him, right? Theremin, did you include him in your master data bank of boys to interview?"

Theremin's eyes flashed. "No, I didn't," he replied. "He wasn't in the dorm when I made the list. They'd moved him to the basement, right?"

"Right!" Newton said. "Come on. We've got to go talk to him. Thanks so much, Tabitha."

"I'm not sure what I did, but you're welcome," Tabitha replied as Newton and his friends ran off.

"I believe he's in the boiler room," Higgy said. "I passed by a big tank in there last night on the way to the cafeteria."

They raced to the basement and followed Higgy to the boiler room. They stepped inside, and everyone gasped.

Odifin had grown even bigger in the previous two days. His brain was now almost the same size as the shark tank. His eyes were the size of beach balls, and his new tendrils of thick brain matter were even longer than before.

He doesn't look like Odifin anymore, Newton thought. Newton's whole body prickled with the warning that danger was near. *He looks like a monster!*

Theremin turned around and rocketed out of the boiler room as fast as he could. Shelly, Newton, and Higgy ran after him.

"We can't just run away!" Shelly told Theremin.

"Of course we can," Theremin replied. "Whatever that thing is, it looks dangerous!"

"He does look like a monster," Newton whispered, so Odifin wouldn't hear.

"Guys, he obviously needs our help," Shelly said.

"I don't think even *you* can help him, Shelly," Theremin said. "We should tell Ms. Mumtaz that he has grown even bigger."

"I agree," Higgy said. "I mean, I know I'm weird and squishy, but that is one enormous weird and squishy bloke!"

"Wait!" Newton said. "We can't tell Ms. Mumtaz," he argued. "She'll send him away. And I need to find out if he's my brother."

"So, what are we going to do?" Theremin asked.

Newton took a deep breath. He tried to quiet the panicked part of his brain that wanted him to camouflage, to disappear, or to flee.

"Not we. *I'm* going to interview him," Newton said. Then he turned and walked back inside the boiler room.

"Hi, Odifin," he said, and the lights in the boiler room flickered off and on.

"Hello, Newton," Odifin replied. "What are you doing here?" Odifin's enormous membranes pulsed in the super bluegoo, and Newton's stomach flip-flopped.

But he kept it together as Shelly, Theremin, and Higgy joined him.

"I, um, I'm interviewing kids for the yearbook," Newton said, which was the cover Shelly had come up with for all the interviews. "Can I ask you a few questions?"

"What kind of questions?" Odifin snapped.

"Personal questions," Newton answered him. "Like,

where you were born and who your family is, stuff like that."

"Aha!" Odifin cried, and the super bluegoo inside the shark tank bubbled and glowed as he accessed the school's mainframe.

"What do you mean, 'aha!'?" Newton asked.

"I know what you're trying to do," Odifin said. "You are not on the yearbook staff. So there can only be one reason why you're asking me these questions."

Newton and his friends were silent. Did Odifin know about Newton's search for his brother?

"I'm now the most famous student Franken-Sci High has ever had!" Odifin said. "So I will surely be a question in the Brilliant Brains Trivia Competition. Well, you aren't going to get anything out of me, so quit trying."

"That's not it at all," Newton said.

Theremin forgot all about his fear of the monster brain. "Do you really think you're going to be a question in the competition? You're not *that* important."

Shelly nudged him. "Theremin!"

"Don't try to fool me, robot boy," Odifin said. "Now leave me alone. You're a distraction, and I need to get back to studying for the competition. Nothing is going to stop me from winning."

"Listen, you're right that the yearbook thing was a

lie, but you've got to let me talk to you," Newton said. "Please. It's important, Odifin."

The lights in the boiler room began to flicker, and the boiler began to groan.

"You all had better leave now, before I get angry," Odifin said. "And you don't want to see me angry, do you?"

"No!" Theremin replied, and bolted out of the boiler room, followed by Higgy. Shelly grabbed Newton by the elbow.

"Come on, Newton," she said. "He wants to be alone."

"Okay," Newton said, but he moved slowly, watching Odifin pulse in the shark tank.

Could my brother really be a giant brain? he wondered. *I guess anything's possible. But now I'll never know!*

CHAPTER 9

Rotwang Reaches Out

A few hours later Newton and his friends were eating dinner in the cafeteria. Shelly munched on a salad, with chickpeas that bounced up and down in the bowl. She concentrated, trying to spear them with her fork.

"Shelly, did you animate those chickpeas?" Theremin asked.

Shelly shook her head. "The cafeteria is working on food that improves your brain and motor skills. Stabbing the jumping chickpeas is increasing my dexterity."

"That looks like way too much work for me," Higgy responded, slurping down a bowl of gummy worms.

"Since when do they serve gummy worms in the cafeteria?" Shelly asked.

"They don't," Higgy replied. "These are from my own personal stash."

Newton stuck his fork into the pile of food on his plate. As usual, he'd just piled on anything that looked good to

him. Today's dinner was mashed potatoes, crushed pineapple, nacho cheese sauce on a jelly doughnut, and two meatballs, all in a pile just the way he liked it.

"So are you guys going to study for the trivia competition tonight?" Newton asked.

"That's the plan," Theremin said. "We don't mean to ditch you, but we're running out of days left to study. And I really want to win this thing!"

"Me too," Higgy added.

Shelly shrugged. "And I just don't want to embarrass myself by getting a bunch of stuff wrong," she said. "The competition is broadcast to mad scientists all over the world. It's very—"

She stopped. "Rotwang, how long have you been standing there?"

Newton turned around to see Rotwang, standing there with his greasy hair over his eyes.

"Ever since Newton put nacho cheese on his jelly donut," Rotwang replied. "You know, everyone in this school looks down on me for being an assistant, but at least I know how to eat."

"Nobody looks . . . down on you," Newton said, but his voice became more unsure with each word. Rotwang wasn't exactly lying. He'd noticed that mad scientists seemed to all think they were superior to assistants.

"What do you want?" Theremin asked.

"I need to talk," Rotwang said. "It's about Odifin." The lights flickered.

"Sure," Shelly said, and Rotwang sat down at the table.

"I'm worried about him," Rotwang said. "I mean, he's always been evil and nasty. But now that he's a giant brain, he's getting out of control. All the weird things happening in the school—I think he's causing them."

"Odifin?" Higgy asked, and the lights flickered again.

"Yeah, like that," Rotwang said. "The lights flicker every time someone says his name. And lockers opening and everything spilling out. The sprinklers going off. Washing machines spinning at super-high speeds. I think *he's* doing it."

"That makes sense," Higgy remarked. "He is likely using his brain waves to connect to the school's technology."

"How would he be able to do that?" Shelly wondered.

"With the super bluegoo," Rotwang replied. "It's loaded with nano particles that transmit wireless energy. His tank is full of it."

Theremin looked at Rotwang. "Okay, interesting. So, why are you asking us to help?" he asked. "Why not ask Mumtaz?"

Rotwang shrugged. "Well, because you guys are, like, smart and stuff," he said. "You won the science fair. You saved the school from that giant monster."

Rotwang was talking about Shelly's monster friend Peewee. He had transformed into a giant beast by accident several weeks before, and had freaked out the school until Shelly had recognized him and Professor Flubitus had changed Peewee back to normal.

"And you're nice," Rotwang continued. "You're not mean to me like other kids are. Well, Theremin is kinda mean, but the rest of you aren't."

Theremin frowned. "Well, you probably deserved it," he said. "And I still think this is a job for Mumtaz, not for us."

Rotwang shook his head. "I don't want her to expel him," he said. "He's my only friend here. And I *am* his friend, even if he doesn't think so."

Only friend, Newton thought. He had Shelly, Theremin, and Higgy, but Odifin and Rotwang only had each other. A feeling of gratitude welled up in Newton. "Well, I think we should try to help him," he said. "It can't be easy being a brain in a jar, or worse, a giant brain in a giant tank. It sounds like things just got out of control."

"I think there's another reason why we should help,"

Higgy said. "He's getting bigger and bigger, right? We're lucky that all he's done is set off some sprinklers and make the lights flash. Just imagine what he could do if he really put his mind to it. He could wipe out all the school's data! He could—"

Rotwang put a hand over Higgy's mouth. "He could be listening," he whispered. "Don't give him any ideas."

Shelly leaned in. "We should go somewhere and talk where there's no technology," she suggested, and turned to Theremin.

Theremin's eyes flashed as he scanned a blueprint of the island in his data banks. "Follow me!"

As they left, Higgy slurped up the remainder of the food on Newton's plate. His friends looked at him.

"What? I can't plot to save the school on an empty stomach," he said.

They made their way out into the jungle between the school and the dorms. The humid air buzzed with insects as the sun set, and Newton, for a reason he didn't understand, felt a strange urge to catch the insects with his tongue. He resisted and tried to ignore the feeling.

"Okay," Shelly said. "So, Odifin is using special goo—"

"Super bluegoo," Rotwang interrupted.

"Super bluegoo," Shelly repeated, "to control all of

the school's technology. And his tank is filled with it?"

Rotwang nodded.

"What would happen if we drained the super blue-goo out of the tank?" Newton asked.

"Well, Odifin wouldn't be able to connect without it," Rotwang replied. "But even if a little bit is stuck to his brain, he'd still be able to connect. And we can't get rid of the super bluegoo, because then he would dry out, which wouldn't be good."

"What kind of goo did he use before?" Theremin asked.

"Regular goo, I guess?" Rotwang said. "His mom sends it here when he's running low. I have a jug of it in our room, but it wouldn't even be enough to *start* to fill up the tank."

"If we can take a sample, we might be able to make more," Higgy suggested as he removed a glove and revealed his jellylike hand. "I am pretty well versed in goo-based chemistry."

Shelly took the lead. "Okay, so what we need to do is get the super bluegoo out of the tank and rinse any trace of it off you-know-who," she said, and then she remembered both that they were out of Odifin's range and that they were outside, where no lights could flicker, so she said his name. "I mean Odifin. Then we will need

to replace the super bluegoo with gallons and gallons of regular goo that we have to make ourselves. Um . . ."

"That all sounds kind of hard," Newton said.

"Well, once Higgy makes new regular goo to replace the super bluegoo," Shelly said, "we just have to drain the tank and rinse off Odifin. How should we do it?"

"We could use buckets and dump the super bluegoo out when he's asleep," Theremin said.

"Does he sleep?" Newton asked.

"He used to," Rotwang replied. "I'm not sure he does anymore."

"There's got to be a way to drain the shark tank," Shelly said, tapping her finger on her chin. "I know big aquarium tanks have drains that can be opened for this sort of thing. Maybe this tank does too."

"Wait. Odifin borrowed the tank from Tori Twitcher," Theremin said. "She used it for the science fair."

"Right! I'll just check the photos I took that day and see if I can find a picture of the tank," Shelly said, and she browsed the photos in her tablet. A few seconds later she grinned. "I see a drain!"

"That's all well and good, but that super bluegoo must be high-quality stuff. If it has great viscosity," Higgy remarked, "it will take a long time to drain. And while it's draining, Odifin might get angry."

Newton pictured the shark tank in his mind. "Maybe we could water down the goo to help flush it out faster," he said. "That would also help us rinse the goo off Odifin."

"Where will we get that much water?" Higgy wondered.

Theremin's eyes glowed. He scrolled through his memory banks to look at the boiler room again. "The boiler room has four sprinklers," he said. "That might be enough to flush the tank."

"Only one problem," Rotwang reminded them. "Odifin can control the school's sprinklers."

"Oh, right!" Shelly frowned. "That's too bad. Otherwise it would have been the perfect solution!"

"Don't feel bad, guys," Rotwang said. "I know you're all smart. But it's hard to be smarter than a big, fat giant brain."

Newton grinned. "We may not be smarter than a giant brain, but do you know what is?" he asked.

Theremin grinned back at him. "A whole lot of brains!"

"Good thinking!" Shelly said. "Let's go to the Brain Bank!"

Drone Attack!

The five of them hurried into the school. By the time they reached the library, Newton was ten steps ahead of everyone else.

Shelly called to him. "Newton, wait up!"

"Sorry," he answered slowly. "It's awfully hot in here, isn't it? I'm feeling really energetic all of a sudden."

Theremin's eyes flashed as he scanned the temperature. "You're right!" he cried. "It's almost one hundred degrees Fahrenheit in here!"

"It's got to be Odifin." The lights flickered again as Shelly spoke, since they were back in range. "He's messing with the heat system."

"Why does the school even have a heat system on a tropical island?" Higgy asked.

"I think it was installed after the invention of the Freeze Ray," Shelly said. "But we're getting off track. We need to find a way to bypass Odifin messing with

the controls and get to the sprinkler system."

"Right," Newton said. "And there's got to be some-body in the Brain Bank who can help us."

When they arrived in the Brain Bank, the eyes of all the brains turned to them. Shelly plugged her tablet into the directory. "Let's see, there's Elvira Mixenhooper, Ignatius Nakamura, Rodena Mezmer—"

"I know that name," Theremin said, interrupting her. "Father always talked about her as being a master pro-grammer. She designed the original technological infra-structure of the school."

"Then let's talk to her," Shelly said.

The lights in the Brain Bank flashed off and on. The school's fire alarm began to sound.

"I think Odifin knows we're up to something," Rotwang said, and the lights flashed again.

"I'll talk to Rodena," Newton offered. "How does it work again?"

"You connect your tablet to her brain port, or use one of the new headsets to talk to her," Shelly suggested. "That might be the easiest way, in this case. You can tell her exactly what we need."

Newton nodded. "Got it," he said. He picked up one of the headsets and walked past the jars of brains until he found the one labeled with the name Rodena

Mezmer. He put the headset over his ears and plugged it into the port on the jar.

"Hello? Ms. Mezmer?" he asked out loud.

Hello, young man. And please, call me "Rodena."

"Hi, Rodena," Newton said. "I'm sorry to ask for your help when I don't even know you, but my friends and I have a favor to ask."

So many favors these days, Rodena said. *But at least you're polite. Unlike that brain who just wanted our knowledge and then disconnected from us all without so much as a thank-you!*

"That's why we're here. We're trying to stop that brain from taking over the school. Can you help us?" Newton asked. "Please? You're the only one who can do it."

Rodena's eyestalks moved up and down as she, seeming to recognize him, looked at Newton. *Say, you're Newton Warp, aren't you?*

"Yes," Newton replied. "How do you know my name?"

We all remember the day you showed up in the Brain Bank, Rodena replied. *Very interesting circumstances. You were right in my line of sight, you see, and . . .* She paused.

Newton felt a burst of hope in his heart. "What did you see?"

Then, from across the room, he heard Shelly cry out. "Newton! Hurry up!"

He turned to see an army of security drones flying toward the Brain Bank. Shelly, Rotwang, Theremin, and Higgy slammed the doors shut and pressed their bodies against them.

"It's Odifin!" Rotwang cried, and the lights flickered. "We need to hurry up and drain his tank!"

"Right," Newton said. "Rodena, it's an emergency. Odifin"—the lights flickered—"is controlling all of the technology running the school, and we need to turn on the boiler room sprinklers to help stop him, but we need your help to keep him from stopping us."

Sounds like that young man is out of control, Rodena said. *But I can help. The original system I created was never dismantled. If you can access the mainframe and log into the Y-Me 2 port, you should be able to turn the sprinklers on from there. Your grumpy robot friend should be able to do that. It should take you-know-who a few minutes before he discovers what you're doing and locates the Y-Me 2 port himself.*

"Got it," Newton said. Then he called out to Theremin. "Theremin, come here." Then he lowered his voice to a whisper and said, "You need to log into the mainframe and find the Y-Me 2 port from the original system Rodena built. You can access the sprinklers from there."

Theremin sped over to a control panel on the wall. A metal rod sprang from his chest and plugged into the panel. "I'm searching for it now. But don't forget, we need to drain the goo from the tank."

"I'm on it!" Higgy said, and he moved away from the door, where the security drones were banging against the glass, trying to get in. He slipped down into a vent in the floor.

"Just give me a minute or two!" he called out as he disappeared.

"Newton, we need help with this door!" Shelly cried.

Newton slipped off the headphones and raced to the door, glancing back at Rodena's brain.

What does she know about the day I came to Franken-Sci High? he wondered. *I'll have to ask her later.*

"I found the Y-Me 2 port!" Theremin cried. "Turning on the sprinklers now."

Bam! Bam! BAM! The drones crashed against the glass doors. The glass began to crack.

"Master, cut it out!" Rotwang yelled, since Odifin seemed to be listening. "We're trying to help you!"

"What do you think will happen if those drones break through?" Newton asked.

"I'm not sure," Shelly replied. "But if anything happens, Newton, I'm glad I'm here with—"

Crash! The drones suddenly lost power and fell to the floor.

"Awesome," Shelly said. "I can't believe Higgy pulled the drain from the tank already."

"Higgy had nothing to do with this," Ms. Mumtaz said, walking through the pile of fallen drones. She kicked them aside with her lime-green stiletto heels as she flung open the doors to the Brain Bank. "I've been trying to figure out how to stop Odifin for days now," she said.

"Hey, did you notice that?" Shelly remarked. "The lights didn't flicker when you said his name, Ms. Mumtaz. He must be weakening. Maybe it's working already!"

"I've been working with the faculty to try to stop him, but he keeps getting smarter and smarter and harder to stop. We did manage to break his connection to the drones just now, but that's all. What did you mean when you said, 'Maybe it's working'?"

"Follow us!" Newton cried.

"Can you explain what's happening on the way?" Ms. Mumtaz asked.

"Sure," Newton said. "We figured out a way to drain the super bluegoo from Odifin's tank. Super bluegoo is allowing Odifin to connect to everything wirelessly. But we needed to access the sprinklers to get rid of the goo, so I talked to Rodena Mezmer about how to access them without Odifin knowing, so we could be a step ahead of him."

"You talked to Rodena?" Mumtaz asked, and her thin eyebrows shot up.

"Yes, and Theremin followed her instructions for how to access the mainframe to turn the basement sprinklers on," Newton said. *And she also hinted that she knows something about the first day I came to the school,* he thought, but he didn't say that out loud.

Mumtaz pursed her lips and nodded. "I hope it works, Newton. I really do."

In the basement they stepped into a sticky river of super bluegoo flowing from the boiler room. Higgy had been able to open the drain!

Stubbins Crouch was not amused. He was standing outside the room, waving a mop at Higgy. "You put that goo stuff back in there, Mr. Vollington!" he was yelling. "This is one mess I am NOT cleaning up!"

Inside the boiler room Higgy was sitting on top of the tank, holding the drain plug. The sprinklers were filling the room with water as the super bluegoo was quickly draining out of the bottom of the tank. Odifin was already smaller than the last time Newton had seen him—and was shrinking every second.

The friends hadn't realized that removing the super bluegoo would also drain Odifin's brain of what he had learned from the Brain Bank, or that he would shrink as a result.

"Stop this right now!" Odifin was yelling through the speaker on his original jar, which was still connected to the shark tank since he needed the data panel to talk. "This isn't funny, Higgy!"

"It's not supposed to be funny, but it has to happen," Higgy replied. He called down to the others. "I never

got a chance to make replacement goo. What's going to happen to Odifin when all the goo is gone?"

"Hold on!" Rotwang cried, and he dashed away, his feet squishing in the super bluegoo as he ran.

"Give me back my super bluegoo!" Odifin yelled. "I WANT MY SUPER BLUEGOO!"

But as the super bluegoo drained away, Odifin shrank smaller and smaller. He began to float in the big shark tank, looking more like a small octopus than a brain. Then his brain tendrils began to shrink too.

Rotwang raced in with a fishing net on a long pole in one hand, and in the other hand he was pushing Odifin's old mechanical rolling table. On top of it was the jug of regular goo he kept in his room.

"I'll save you, Master!" Rotwang cried. He climbed up the tank, scooped Odifin out with the fishing net, and asked Theremin to use his telescoping arm to grab Odifin's original jar from where it was attached to the tank. Then Rotwang carefully poured the regular goo into the jar, disconnected the jar from the tank, and used the net to deposit Odifin into the jar with a gentle *plop!*

"It's good to see you back to normal," Rotwang said with a smile.

Odifin's eyes twitched as he gazed around the basement, and Newton thought he looked dazed.

"I don't want to be normal," Odifin said. "I want to be smart! The smartest boy in the world! All that knowledge—it drained away with the super bluegoo! You've ruined my chances of winning the trivia competition!"

"Is *that* what this was about?" Ms. Mumtaz asked. She shook her head. "Hmph. I never knew you were so competitive, Odifin."

"It doesn't matter," Odifin said. "I'll never win now."

Ms. Mumtaz looked down at her shoes. "Well, this has been an interesting day," she said. "Now I must go take care of a few things. And order some new shoes. Stubbins, would you please get started with cleaning this mess up?"

The custodian grumbled.

"Thank you so much," Ms. Mumtaz added. "I know this is above and beyond your normal scope of work."

Meanwhile, Odifin was eager to leave. "Come, Rotwang," Odifin said. "I want to go back to our room."

Shelly stepped in front of them. "Odifin, why don't you join our study group?" she asked.

"Shelly, you know what he's like!" Theremin hissed.

"No, I mean it," Shelly said. "Winning must mean a whole lot to you, for you to go through all this. And we've been studying almost every night. It's much better studying together. And we were going to head to the library before . . . all this happened. We can go

now and get at least an hour of studying in."

"Yeah, come with us, Odifin," Higgy offered. "It'll be fun."

"Fun?" Odifin asked. "You want me to . . . have fun with you?"

"I'm not sure how much fun it will be," Theremin said. "But sure, I guess. Why not?"

"I'll go too," Newton said.

Shelly turned to Newton and whispered, "I thought you weren't competing."

"I'm not. I need to go back to the Brain Bank to ask Rodena Mezmer a question," he whispered back. "And also, I didn't get a chance to interview Odifin yet."

Shelly nodded.

"Plus, it'll be fun to hang out, even if I'm just helping you guys study," Newton added in a louder voice. "What do you think, Odifin?"

Odifin looked like he was struggling to decide, but then he thought of his mother wanting him to have friends, and he decided to give the kids a chance. "I will . . . I will go with you," Odifin said. Then he turned to Rotwang. "What do you say, Rotwang?"

"Sure," Rotwang said. "If you want me there."

"Of course I do," Odifin said.

They moved to the nearest transport tube and stepped

inside. Newton stood next to Odifin.

"So, Odifin, is it okay if I ask you some of those questions I tried to ask you earlier today?" he asked.

"I don't see why not," Odifin said. "I guess I'm not going to be a question in the competition anymore. Funny, I'm not sure where I got that idea."

"You get a lot of ideas when you're a giant brain, I guess," Rotwang remarked.

"Yeah, I guess so," Odifin said.

"So, um, Odifin," Newton said. "Where were you born?"

"I don't know," Odifin replied. "My mom adopted me. She picked me up here at the school when I was a baby brain."

Newton gasped, and Shelly, Theremin, and Higgy turned around to look at him, because they'd heard the word "adopted" too. If Odifin was adopted, they thought it might be possible that he could be Newton's biological brother without knowing it.

"Do you know anything about your birth parents, or why you're, um, a brain in a jar?" Newton asked.

"No, I don't," Odifin replied. "But you know, it never really mattered to me when I was growing up. Mom always said that choosing me was the best thing she'd ever done, and that we were meant to be family."

"That's amazing," Newton said, and he felt a little pang of jealousy for a mom he'd either never had or couldn't remember. Then Newton's mind began to race as he reviewed what he had just learned. Odifin didn't know anything about his birth family, just like Newton didn't know anything about his parents. Odifin's first moments were at Franken-Sci High, and Newton first showed up at Franken-Sci High. Odifin didn't know why he was a brain in a jar. Newton didn't know why he had strange abilities.

Odifin looked at Newton. "Why are you asking me all this? I thought we were going to the library to study!"

"Odifin, I think you might be my brother," Newton blurted out.

"Is this some kind of joke?" Odifin asked.

"No, no, I'm serious," Newton protested. "You know that I just appeared here in the school one day, right? And I've been trying to find out where I came from, and Professor Flubitus told me I have a relative at the school, and then I found out that my relative is a brother. And since you don't know where you came from either—"

"And I don't care about where I come from," Odifin snapped. "I had a nice life with my mother, until I came to this school. She's all that I need."

"But aren't you curious about your birth parents,

just a little bit?" Newton asked.

Odifin's eyestalks turned so he could stare right at Newton. "If *you* were a brain in a jar, would you want to know how that happened? I'd rather just remember the happy times with my mom."

"I'm not a brain in a jar, but I'm—" Newton began, and then he stopped because Shelly nudged him and gave him a warning glance. He knew what she was probably thinking. It was too soon to trust Odifin with the secret of all of Newton's special abilities. Newton sighed. "I understand, Odifin, I guess," he said.

The transport tube doors opened, and they made their way to the library. It was back to normal. They noticed that the temperature was a perfect 70.3 degrees. The lights weren't flickering, lockers weren't opening on their own, and the crashed drones had been removed.

Odifin, Rotwang, Shelly, Theremin, and Higgy settled around a library table.

"I'll be right back," Newton said, and he entered the Brain Bank. There he picked up a headset and plugged back in to talk with Rodena Mezmer's brain.

"It's me again. Newton," he said.

Hello, my boy, she replied. *It appears as though you were successful in stopping Odifin.*

"Yes, it sure is. Thank you so much, Rodena,"

Newton said. "He's back to his old self now."

Excellent! she said.

"So, I wanted to ask you about the day I woke up in the Brain Bank," Newton said.

Right, Rodena replied. *You were—hmm.* She paused. *This is interesting. I remember seeing you, but I don't remember anything else about that day at all! If I didn't know better, I would say that someone wiped it from my memory banks.*

"Mumtaz," Newton muttered, and he sighed. "Thanks, Rodena."

You're welcome, Newton, she replied. *Come back and visit me anytime.*

Newton sank down to the floor. It was another disappointment. Odifin could be his brother, but he'd never know for sure, because Mumtaz didn't want him to know, and Odifin didn't care enough to find out. It wasn't fair!

"Hey, Newton, get over here!" Theremin called out. "Higgy bet me that I can't balance twelve books on my head, and I'm up to thirteen!"

Newton stood up. One day soon, he hoped he would know the truth about his family. For now, though, he had his friends at least. They were more of a family to him than Odifin might ever be.

CHAPTER 11

Teams Stick Together

"This question's for Newton," Theremin said. "Who was the first mad scientist to create a thunderstorm generator?"

Newton bit his lip, thinking. "Um . . . Ludicrous Kilowatt?"

"Wrong! It's *Ludwig* Kilowatt," Theremin replied.

Odifin laughed. "You know what's ludicrous? Your answer to that question, Newton!"

"Odifin, be nice!" Shelly said. "Newton's trying."

Newton, Shelly, Theremin, Odifin, Rotwang, and Higgy were in the library studying for the Brilliant Brains Trivia Competition, like they had every night for the last week. A few days before, Shelly had suggested that Newton and Rotwang sign up for the competition after all, since they were studying so much anyway. Newton agreed because he wanted to keep getting to know Odifin. Rotwang was thrilled to be competing,

but Odifin made it clear he didn't think *either* of them was a threat to his chances of winning.

"I'm sorry, Newton, but I have to say I don't understand why you're not getting more of these questions right," Odifin said. "I've seen you answer questions like some kind of genius in class. Which makes me think that my theory was correct: you've been cheating somehow."

Newton paused. He still hadn't told Odifin about all of his strange abilities, including the "noodle noggin" thing. "It's hard to explain, Odifin," Newton said. "Sometimes I know the answers, and sometimes I don't. But I'm not cheating."

"Newton would never cheat," Shelly added. "He's not like that."

"Okay, okay," Odifin said. "I take it back. You're not a cheater. You're just not very smart."

But Newton heard a teasing tone in Odifin's mechanical voice, and he grinned. "Yeah, well, I'm working on it."

Just then Tabitha Talos walked by with her nose in a book. She didn't see Odifin and tripped over the wheels of his small transport table. This sent Odifin skidding across the library.

"Rotwang, help!" Odifin cried.

Rotwang jumped up and caught up to Odifin, grabbing the rolling table with one hand. Then Rotwang

steered it back to where the group was studying. The mishap had joggled Odifin's eyeballs around, so that one was sitting on top of the other.

Newton, Shelly, Higgy, and Theremin started to giggle.

"What's so funny?" Odifin asked. "It's not my fault Tabitha tripped."

Theremin took a quick snap of Odifin with his tablet and then showed the photo to Odifin. "This is what's funny," he said.

"Yeah, it sure is," Newton said. "Now, that's what *I'd* call ludicrous."

Odifin moved his eyestalks and put his eyes in the correct position. "I guess that was kind of funny," he admitted.

"You know what's funny?" they heard someone ask. "That you losers think you have a chance of winning the Brilliant Brains Trivia Competition." They all turned to see Mimi Crowninshield standing there with her arms crossed.

"We won the science fair, so I don't think you can call us losers," Theremin pointed out.

"Yeah, and why are you so obsessed with us, anyway?" Shelly asked.

Mimi's cheeks turned pink. "I am *not* obsessed," she said. "I'm talking to you because nobody else is entering the competition."

"What do you mean?" Shelly asked. "I thought almost everybody in the school was entering."

"They were, until Odifin here became a gigant-o brain-o," Mimi sneered. "The rumor is that he knows everything there is to know in the universe. So most people chickened out. Except for me. I'm not afraid of some dumb brain."

"I am not dumb," Odifin said. "And it's true, for a brief moment I possessed all the knowledge the school has to offer. But that all went away when I shrank."

Mimi shrugged. "Doesn't matter to me. Now I only have to beat six of you."

Suddenly the huge holographic head of Headmistress Mumtaz appeared above the middle of the table.

"Mimi, Newton, Shelly, Odifin, Higgy, Theremin, Rotwang," she said. "I want to see you all in my office right now."

The other kids in the library looked up.

"What do you think she wants?" Higgy asked.

"You guys are probably in trouble—as usual," Mimi guessed. "And I was just in the wrong place at the wrong time. I'll straighten it out with Ms. Mumtaz."

They made their way to the office of the headmistress and took seats around her desk—all except for Odifin, who observed from his jar, perched next to Rotwang.

Ms. Mumtaz gazed at them all with her bright green eyes. "Let me explain why I've brought you here," she began. "Since you seven are the only ones still signed up for the trivia competition, I'm going to cancel it."

Mimi stood up. "What? That's not fair!"

"Yeah," the others agreed.

"I have no choice," Ms. Mumtaz said. "Mimi, you know what a big deal this competition is. Mad scientists the world over tune in to watch. It's a major event—a spectacle. You can't have a spectacle with only seven

contestants. We usually have a hundred kids in the first knockout round, before the pack gets narrowed down. That's what the audience wants to see."

"It's Odifin's fault!" Mimi cried, pointing. "All the other kids got scared off because they think he knows everything."

"I've already explained to you that that's not true," Odifin said.

Ms. Mumtaz frowned. "And I suppose there's no trying to assure the students that you're back to normal," she said. "I know what happens when rumors start in this school."

Odifin sighed. "I'll drop out," he said. "Then the other kids won't be afraid to compete."

"No!" Newton cried. "That's not fair."

"That sounds fair to me," Mimi said.

"You guys have all been studying hard," Odifin said. "I'm not going to let my team down."

"That's it!" Newton cried. "Teams!" He stood up and slammed his hands onto Ms. Mumtaz's desk in his excitement. "Change the competition so it has groups competing," he said. "Kids will feel more confident working in teams."

Ms. Mumtaz nodded. "That just might work. It's good to mix things up a bit, offer something new."

Then she frowned. "But we've got only one set of encyclopedias to give away. It would be nice to have one winner."

"You could narrow down the groups in a series of matches until there are only two groups left," Newton suggested. "And then the remaining individual members could compete."

"A final, electrifying lightning round!" Ms. Mumtaz said. "I don't just like it; I LOVE IT! I'll send out a nano-email blast. You are all dismissed."

Mimi stood up and pushed her way through the others to get out.

"What's the rush, Mimi?" Shelly asked.

"I'm going to put a team together," she said, before dashing off.

Shelly turned to Odifin. "That was nice of you, to offer to drop out like that."

"Well, that's what friends do, right?" Odifin asked.

Shelly grinned. "Yeah, that's what friends do."

Theremin slapped Newton on the back. "And that was pretty smart thinking, Newton. The team idea is a good one."

"Thanks," Newton said.

"Yeah, looks like you're pretty smart after all, Newton," Odifin said.

Newton looked around at his friends. "So, I guess we're a team, then, right?"

Rotwang raised an eyebrow. "Even me?"

"Why not you, Rotwang?" Higgy said. "You've been studying with us."

"Cool," Rotwang said, and beamed.

"We need a name for our team," Theremin said. "Something cool. Like 'Team Mega-Smart.'"

"'Team Uber-Undefeated,'" Rotwang suggested.

"But, Rotwang, how can we be undefeated if we've never— Never mind," Odifin said. "I think 'Odifin's Army' has a nice ring to it."

"'The Mighty Monsters,'" Shelly said.

Newton shrugged. "I don't know. Um, 'the Six Students'?"

"It needs to be catchy," Higgy said. "How about 'the Goo Getters'?"

Shelly giggled. "Goo Getters?"

"You know, because of all the goo and stuff," Higgy said. "And, um, goo makes teams stick together, right?"

"I like it," Rotwang said, running a hand through his greasy hair.

"I still like 'Odifin's Army,'" Odifin said.

"Everyone who likes 'Goo Getters,' raise your hand," Shelly called out.

Everyone except for Odifin raised their hand.

"No fair! I don't have hands!" he yelled.

"You can say 'yes' instead of raising a hand," Shelly suggested.

"No," Odifin said.

"Sorry, Odifin," Shelly said, "but you're outnumbered. It's five yeses against one no."

"It's okay," Odifin said. "I guess we can be the Goo Getters."

"Three cheers for the Goo Getters!" Theremin shouted.

The six friends chanted in unison.

"Goo Getters, Goo Getters, Goo Getters!"

CHAPTER 12

Go, Goo Getters!

All was pitch black. Then Ms. Mumtaz's voice rang out.

"Good evening, one and all!"

A crowd cheered in the dark. Then a thousand lights blinked on, revealing that the headmistress was standing in the middle of a triangular platform at the center of an enormous outdoor stadium. Her image appeared on giant screens that could be seen from every seat.

"Welcome to the Seventy-First Annual Franken-Sci High Brilliant Brains Trivia Competition!" Ms. Mumtaz announced. As she spoke, fireworks appeared above the stadium, and shiny drones dropped confetti on the students, professors, and onlookers sitting in the stands.

Newton had first seen the impressive stadium about an hour before, when he and his friends had reported there early. The glass-and-metal structure rose out of the jungle like a massive jewel, and he'd gasped.

"Has this always been here?" he'd asked.

"It's protected by stealth camouflage technology when it's not being used," Theremin had explained. "It draws too much attention to the island otherwise."

They had been met by some upperclassmen who'd ushered them underneath the stadium. Robotic powder puffs had slapped makeup onto all their faces, even Theremin's, and onto Odifin's jar (which Rotwang had dutifully wiped off), and then they'd been told to stand on a red circle. There were a few dozen other kids down there too, getting ready for their introductions.

In the stadium above, the hubbub quieted down when Ms. Mumtaz's voice again echoed through the speakers.

"Tonight we are pleased to have a record five thousand eight hundred and seven mad scientists watching

us from around the world, in nine of the fifty-one dimensions, and even on a few uncharted planets," she continued. "And this year we're making history with a brand-new format: teams!"

The crowd cheered.

"First up," Mumtaz announced, "is a team of freshmen friends including an assistant, a brain, a robot, a jokester, a monster maker, and a boy with amnesia. It's the Goo Getters!"

The group's red circle platform rose to the ceiling, where a circular hole swirled open. Odifin and his table almost rolled off as the platform was lifted high into the air, and Rotwang grabbed them just in time.

Boom! Boom! Boom! More fireworks exploded overhead, and Newton flinched. He had to concentrate to keep from camouflaging himself out of fear, but it wasn't easy to keep his cool. Drone cameras looped and whirred around them, bright lights shone into their eyes, and the sight of the crowded stands made the hair on the back of his neck stand up.

The fireworks continued as more teams were announced: Mimi and her team, the Destroyers; a group of seniors calling themselves the Invincibles; Team Myopia was a group of kids all wearing glasses; and there was one last team, the Rowdy Rebels.

"The format has changed, but the rules are simple," Ms. Mumtaz said. "Each team is asked a question. One wrong answer, and they're out. We'll keep asking questions until there are two teams left. Then those team members will compete individually.

"In the event that any answers are challenged, our judges will make the final determination," she said, and she pointed to a box floating nearby. "Welcome, Professor Leviathan, Professor Phlegm, and Professor Wagg!"

The cameras swung around and closed in on them. Leviathan with her wild, curly hair cried out "Woot, woot!" Phlegm snarled at the camera. And ancient Professor Wagg, asleep as usual, snored.

"Before we begin, I'd like to thank tonight's sponsor, Crowninshield Industries," Ms. Mumtaz continued, "makers of the DNA-in-a-Snap kit. It's DNA testing without the muss and fuss!"

A colorful box with the words "DNA-in-a-Snap" appeared on the screen. In the corner of the box was a logo with a golden crown and the name "Crowninshield."

"Our winner tonight will get a complete set of the Encyclopedia of Mad Scientists," Mumtaz went on. "Plus, a giant holographic statue of the winner will be projected in the school's Center Court for one week.

Teams, are we ready to get started?"

"Yes!" Newton cheered, along with the others. He felt excited. He'd been studying extra hard for this event, because he didn't want to embarrass himself if his team made it to the individual round.

He looked at his friends. Rotwang was sweating. Odifin's eyes were gazing all around the stadium. Shelly had her eyes closed, calming herself. Theremin was literally sparking with excitement, and Higgy was rocking back and forth, making farting noises with his feet and cracking up everyone in the stands.

One of the camera drones settled in front of them.

"Our first question is for Team Goo Getters," Ms. Mumtaz said, and the stadium got quiet.

"What are the Cartesian coordinates?" she asked. "You have ten seconds to answer."

For the first question, it was a tough one. A red number ten appeared on all the screens and began to count down.

Newton searched his brain but came up with nothing.

"Are those related to geography?" Shelly asked the other team members.

Theremin's eyes flashed with excitement. "It's more about location in general. They're used in robotics!" he said. "I got this. Trust me."

The drone camera zoomed in front of Theremin as he answered.

"Cartesian coordinates are a system that uses a pair of numbers, or coordinates, to specify the location of a point in a two-dimensional space," Theremin said.

"Correct!" Ms. Mumtaz announced, and a cheer went up from the stands. Newton patted Theremin on the back.

"Way to go, ro-bro!" he said.

"Destroyers, it's your turn," Mumtaz said. "Here is your question: Who created the first formula for artificial happiness?"

I know this one, Newton thought as he watched Mimi and her team huddle together. *It's Gladiolus—*

"Gladiolus Farfengiggle," Mimi said confidently.

"Correct!" Mumtaz said. "Now on to the Invincibles! Here is your question: What is the name of the transportation particle discovered by Professor Yuptuka?"

The students huddled. Newton realized he knew this one too. He waited to see if the Invincibles would get it right.

"Um, a quicksicle?" answered a purple-haired boy as the buzzer went off.

"Incorrect! The correct answer is a bouncicle,"

Ms. Mumtaz said. "Sorry, Invincibles. Bye-bye!"

Whoosh! The Invincibles' platform quickly dropped through the stadium floor and disappeared. The team would join the rest of the spectators in the stands to watch the remainder of the competition.

"And then there were four!" Mumtaz said.

Next the kids in Team Myopia answered a question about unstable elements correctly. Then it was the Rowdy Rebels' turn. Mumtaz asked them who the father of vegetable animation was.

The leader of the Rowdy Rebels answered Ms. Mumtaz in a whisper. "Phineas Broccolini?" he said, barely audibly.

"Can you repeat that, please?" Mumtaz asked. "A little louder?"

"Phineas Broccolini," the boy repeated.

"LOUDER, please!" Mumtaz shouted.

"Phineas Broccolini," the boy replied in a normal speaking voice, and his answer could finally be heard by Mumtaz.

"Correct!" Ms. Mumtaz said. "But I'm changing your name to the Not-So-Rowdy Rebels! Back to you, Team Goo Getters!"

The next question was about monsters, and Shelly got it right. Then the Destroyers got their question

right. So did Team Myopia and the Not-So-Rowdy Rebels.

"There are still four!" Mumtaz announced, and the stadium filled with cheers.

The competition heated up as the teams got one correct answer after another. Then Mumtaz asked the Not-So-Rowdy-Rebels, "Which animal is faster, a Brazilian spider beetle or a Tasmanian temporal sloth?"

It's a trick question, Newton thought. *You might think it's the spider beetle because sloths are slow, but—*

"The Brazilian spider beetle," answered the Not-So-Rowdy team leader.

"Incorrect!" Ms. Mumtaz said. "The temporal sloth is faster because it can travel through time. But good try! Let's hear it for the Not-So-Rowdy Rebels!"

Everyone cheered as the Rebels sank down through the floor and out of sight.

"Your turn, Goo Getters," Ms. Mumtaz said. "What was the first animal to be brought back to life with lightning?"

The Goo Getters huddled.

"I should know this," Shelly said. "I'm pretty sure it was a worm."

"No, I remember this," Newton said. "It's a frog."

"A frog. Newton is right," Odifin agreed.

They broke the huddle. Newton stared into the camera drone and took a deep breath. "A frog?" he answered confidently.

"Correct!" Mumtaz replied. "Nicely done, Goo Getters. Destroyers, you must get this next question right, or the Goo Getters and Team Myopia are going to the individual round."

"We will get it right," Mimi promised, and she was right—they did.

Then Team Myopia got their next question wrong.

"Good try, Team Myopia!" Mumtaz said as the disappointed, bespectacled team sank into the floor.

Theremin nudged Newton. "We did it! We're moving on to the next round!"

"Now it's time for the individual round," Ms. Mumtaz announced. "Each member of the two teams will now compete against all remaining contestants. Contestants, get ready!"

Twelve small, individual pillars rose from the floor. Drones swept in and lifted each of the remaining contestants with mechanical hands. Newton's heart pounded as his drone carried him across the stadium to one of the small pillars. The drones deposited Odifin on the pillar to Newton's left, and Theremin on the pillar to his right.

He looked across at the members of the Destroyers team: Mimi, Tabitha Talos, Debbie Danning, Faraday Michaels, Archimedes Jones, and Boris Bacon.

That's a lot of kids to beat, Newton thought. *But I'm glad I made it this far!*

"The rules are basically the same," Ms. Mumtaz said. "If you get a question wrong, you will be eliminated. The last student standing is the winner. But the final two competitors will get the option to call a family member if they need help with an answer."

The audience murmured with excitement.

"Up first is Rotwang," Mumtaz announced.

Newton heard a few snickers in the crowd. He looked over at Rotwang, whom he now thought of as a friend. Rotwang hadn't gotten many questions right in practice.

I feel bad for him! Newton thought. *When he gets eliminated first, everyone's going to say it's because he's an assistant.*

"You can do it, Rotwang!" Odifin called out.

"Rotwang, who was the lab assistant to the famous mad scientist Jann von Hoppenheimer?" Mumtaz asked.

Rotwang beamed. "Finster Snivers! He was my great-great-uncle!"

"Correct!" Ms. Mumtaz said. "Well done, Rotwang.

149

All right, Shelly, here's your question: How many horns does the three-horned flying cave creature have?"

Mimi spoke up. "I object! That is an unfair question. The answer is right in the question. It's three horns, obviously."

"You're wrong, Mimi," Shelly said calmly. "A three-horned flying cave creature has a hidden horn on the roof of its mouth. So the answer is four."

"Correct, Shelly!" Ms. Mumtaz said. "And, Mimi, because you got the question wrong, you are eliminated."

"Wait, that's double unfair!" Mimi yelled. "It wasn't my question; it was Shelly's."

"Judges, what say you?" Ms. Mumtaz asked.

Professor Phlegm nudged Professor Wagg awake. Then the three judges huddled, and Professor Leviathan stood up.

"The rules are simple. You are eliminated if you get a question wrong," she said in her booming voice. "The rules don't say which question. So, Mimi, you are eliminated!"

"Noooooooooo!" Mimi wailed as her pillar descended into the floor.

The rests of the contestants breathed a sigh of relief, grateful not to be the first eliminated. But more questions and eliminations quickly followed. Higgy got a

question wrong about the invention of solar-powered eyebrows. Tabitha missed the next one. Odifin and Theremin each got their first question right, and then it was Newton's turn.

"Newton, which mineral, when used as a powder, can cure dimension sickness?" Ms. Mumtaz asked.

The answer popped into Newton's head. "Stablesium!" he said.

"Correct!" Ms. Mumtaz said, and the crowd cheered.

The questions came faster. Rotwang missed a question and was eliminated, and then nobody got a question wrong for two rounds in a row. But the third round wiped out Archimedes and Faraday. Then Shelly missed a physics question, and Newton's heart fell as he watched her descend through the stage below.

"Go get them, Goo Getters!" she called out with a smile.

And then there were four: Debbie, Theremin, Odifin, and Newton.

"Theremin, who can eat more hot dogs in five minutes? An average third grader or a carnivorous carnation?" Mumtaz asked.

"Um, the third grader?" Theremin guessed.

"Incorrect!" Ms. Mumtaz said. "A carnivorous carnation can eat forty-seven hot dogs in five minutes, but

experiments with third graders showed an average of only thirteen."

Theremin's eyes glowed red. "What kind of a dumb question is—"

Whoosh! His pillar sank down into the floor.

"Debbie, name two ingredients in Professor Draconus Node's classic formula for improving memory," Ms. Mumtaz said.

Debbie bit her lip, concentrating. Newton could see beads of sweat forming on her forehead.

"Magnesium and . . . barium?" she said tentatively.

"The correct answer is magnesium and grape jelly," Ms. Mumtaz said, and Debbie disappeared. "That leaves us with our two finalists: Newton Warp and Odifin Pinkwad!"

The stadium filled with applause.

I can't believe it, Newton thought. The cheers coming from the crowd made him feel warm inside in a way he'd never felt before. *I'm . . . I'm good at this!*

"All right, Newton. This question is for you," Ms. Mumtaz said. "Name the five changing states of theoretical matter."

Newton searched his brain. He remembered reading about this, but he wasn't sure if he could name all five. "Instigation," he said slowly. "Disintegration.

Destruction. Combustion. And . . ."

He stopped. *Gasp!* He couldn't think of the fifth state.

"Newton, remember that you have the option to call a family member for help," Ms. Mumtaz said, and her face fell as she said it. She knew as well as Newton that he had no one to call.

"No, that's okay," Newton said, trying not to let on how sad that had made him. He took a wild guess. "Computation?"

"Incorrect. The correct answer is mutation," she said.

Newton prepared himself for the plunge down through the stage.

"But you're not going anywhere yet," Mumtaz added. "If Odifin gets his question wrong, you'll still have a chance to win."

Newton nodded.

"Are you ready, Odifin?" Ms. Mumtaz asked.

"Ready," he said.

"Here's your question," she said. "Who was the first mad scientist to create a thunderstorm generator?"

CHAPTER 13

A Ludicrous Question

Odifin's eyestalks swung around to look at Newton, who was grinning at him happily. Odifin wished he could smile back at Newton.

"It's rather a *ludicrous* question," Odifin said, and Newton started laughing at their shared joke. "I'd like to call my mom, please."

"Certainly," said Ms. Mumtaz, and the sound of numbers being dialed echoed through the stadium.

"Hello?"

"Hi, Mom. It's me."

"You're doing so great, Odifin!" his mom said. "I'm so proud of you. And you look so handsome on television."

"Thirty seconds, Odifin," Ms. Mumtaz warned. "Ask her the question."

"Mom, I just want to say I'm sorry I lied to you," Odifin began.

"Apology accepted, Odie," Ms. Pinkwad replied. "I know you were under a lot of stress."

"And I don't want you to worry about me," Odifin said. "I'm glad you sent me to Franken-Sci High."

"You're sure you're not lonely?" his mom asked.

"No, Mom," Odifin said. He looked over at Newton. "I've got friends now. Real friends."

"I'm glad to hear that—" Ms. Pinkwad said, but she was interrupted by Ms. Mumtaz saying "Ahem."

"Time's up, Odifin!" Ms. Mumtaz said. "And while that was a very interesting phone call, I need your answer. Who was the first mad scientist to create a thunderstorm generator?"

"Ludwig Kilowatt," Odifin said.

"That answer is . . . CORRECT!" Ms. Mumtaz said. "Congratulations, Odifin Pinkwad! You are the winner of the Brilliant Brains Trivia Competition!"

Boom! Boom! BOOM! The sky filled with fireworks, and more sparkling confetti fell from the drones flying above.

A camera drone zoomed in on Odifin's jar.

"Odifin, is there anything you'd like to say?" Ms. Mumtaz asked.

"Yes," he said. "Goo Getters, meet me in my room. It's time to party!"

CHAPTER 14

DNA in a Snap!

"Odifin! Odifin!" Newton cheered. He didn't mind losing, not one bit. It was great to see Odifin so happy.

A drone flew in and lifted Newton again. It gently deposited him onto Ms. Mumtaz's platform, right next to her.

"Well done, Newton," Ms. Mumtaz said. "I know you studied hard for today."

"I did," Newton said.

She handed him a box. "Here. This is the prize for the runner-up."

Newton looked at the box in his hands. It was the DNA-in-a-Snap kit from Crowninshield Industries.

"Um, thanks," he said.

"You never know when a DNA kit might come in handy," she said. And Newton wasn't sure, but he thought she winked at him. Or was it just a blink?

Then he remembered. His friends had said he could

use a DNA test to figure out if Odifin was really his brother or not.

"Thanks," he said again, but his excitement quickly fizzled, because he remembered that Odifin didn't want to know if they were brothers.

Still, he tucked the box under his arm and made his way through the crowds of students back to the dorm. It took him a while because, as he walked, kids kept congratulating him.

"You were great up there, Newton!"

"Nice job, Newton!"

"Way to go, Newton!"

In the boys' dorm he found Shelly, Theremin, Rotwang, and Higgy crowded together inside Odifin and Rotwang's room. The 753 volumes of the encyclopedia set had already been transported there, and there wasn't much room to stand.

Shelly hugged him. "I'm so proud of you, Newton!"

"Thanks," he said. "But I'm really happy for Odifin. He brought it home for the Goo Getters!"

Odifin wheeled into the room. "Sorry I'm late," he said. "I had to speak to some reporters. Wow, look at these encyclopedias!"

"Yes, what a great prize," Higgy said a little sadly.

"Higgy, you can come over and read or borrow

them anytime you want," Odifin promised.

"I won something too," Newton said, and he held out the DNA kit.

"Hey, that's perfect!" Theremin said. "You can use it on you and Odifin."

"I would," Newton began, "but Odifin doesn't want—"

"Bring on the test!" Odifin said.

"Really?" Newton asked.

"Absolutely," Odifin said. "I realized tonight, when you didn't have any relatives to call, how hard it must be for you not to have any family at all. At least I have my mom. If we turn out to be brothers, at least you'll have me. And my mom can be your family too."

Newton beamed at him. "Thank you, Odifin!" he said, and then he thought nervously, *What if the test shows we aren't brothers?* The thought was too upsetting, so he pushed it out of his head.

Theremin opened the box and pulled out a pair of goggles made of clear plastic.

"So, when you wear these goggles, they'll take a picture of the DNA strands floating in the cells of your and Odifin's eyes. The pictures are uploaded to a phone or computer. Then you use the Crowninshield app to instantly compare them."

"I'll download the app for you, Newton," Shelly offered. "Give me your tablet."

Newton handed it over while Theremin adjusted the strap on the goggles. Then Newton placed the goggles over his eyes, and the room brightened with a bright flash.

"Okay. The picture is uploading," Shelly said.

"Me next!" Odifin said.

Newton handed the goggles to Rotwang, who held them up to Odifin's eyes. A second flash filled the room with light.

"Okay. The app is processing the data," Shelly reported.

The room got quiet as they waited for the results.

"You know it won't matter what the results are," Odifin said as he rolled closer to Newton. "You can still be my brother if you want."

"Hey, Odifin, you're already my almost-brother," Theremin put in.

"And mine," Higgy said.

"And mine," Shelly added.

"I'll be your brother too, if you want me," Rotwang offered as he too moved closer to Newton.

"Thanks, everybody," Newton said. "It means a lot to me. I may never find my family, but—" His tablet

pinged. Shelly looked at the screen, and her eyes got wide.

"Well?" Newton asked.

"What are the results?" Odifin said.

"It says here that you're more closely related than first cousins, but less close than brothers," Shelly responded.

Newton frowned. "What's between a first cousin and a brother?"

"I'm not sure," Shelly admitted. "But I think it's good news. You two are definitely related!"

Newton looked at Odifin. "Definitely?" he asked.

Shelly put her arms around Newton and Odifin's jar. "Double definitely," Shelly said. "But if I were you, I'd show this to Professor Flubitus. He can't ignore a DNA test."

"Right," Newton said as he took the tablet from her. "Do you want to come with me, Odifin?"

"Sure, almost-bro," Odifin joked. "The rest of you can stay here and have fun."

"Great!" Higgy shouted. "I'm going to dive into the encyclopedia volume twenty-seven. It's all about bizarre diseases!"

Newton and Odifin went back to the main school building.

"So we're related," Newton sighed.

"Apparently we are," Odifin replied.

There was an awkward silence, but Newton was smiling.

"You know, maybe this means you can come home with me for the holidays," Odifin said. "Mom makes a great pumpkin pie. I mean, I've never eaten it, but it looks amazing."

"That would be really nice," Newton said, and that warm, fuzzy feeling filled his heart again.

They found Professor Flubitus in his office, watching cartoons on his laptop. He slammed it shut when the boys entered.

"Newton. Odifin. What brings you here . . . together?" he asked, a little bit nervously.

Newton held out the tablet. "We did a DNA test," he said. "So we know we're related."

Flubitus looked at the tablet and ran his fingers through his green hair. "Very impressive," he said. "You've figured it out."

"Figured out what, exactly?" Newton pressed.

"You boys are brothers," Flubitus said. "Half brothers, technically."

Newton stepped forward. "So, tell us more."

"I'm afraid I can't," Flubitus said.

"Newton, it's okay," Odifin said. "I mean, we've got

the DNA test to prove it. And now Flubitus confirms it. We're brothers! I've always wanted a brother."

Odifin was right. Now that Flubitus had confirmed it, Newton felt like he could really celebrate. "I wanted to find my family. And here you are."

Flubitus stood up. "Lovely. Now run along, boys! And no more questions!"

Newton and Odifin moved to the hallway, and Odifin stopped.

"Newton, are you—are you glad it's me?" Odifin asked.

"Sure," Newton replied. "Why wouldn't I be?"

"Well, until recently we weren't even friends," Odifin said. "I'm still not sure why you and your friends asked me to join your study group. After all that happened between us."

"Well, like you, I know what it's like to lose control sometimes," Newton admitted. "We just wanted to help you. And it turned out to be awesome."

"Yes, it did," Odifin said. "What do you mean, though, about losing control?"

"It's a long story," Newton said as they headed back to Odifin's room. "I guess we have a lot to learn from each other."

"Yes," Odifin said. "For example, do you sleep with

a night-light on? Because I always have."

"No," Newton answered. "But I see pretty well in the dark."

"What's your favorite color?" Odifin asked.

"Um, green," Newton responded.

"ME TOO!" Odifin said. "I'm sure we'll have a bazillion things to ask each other. Like, I wonder which one of us is older. Not that it matters, but I've always wanted a little brother . . ."

Newton looked at Odifin as he chatted away. Newton was excited to feel hope rising inside him. *Things are changing,* he realized. *Odifin used to be mean, and now look at him! And look at me. I used to not have any family, and now I have a half brother.*

Yes, it was strange that Newton's half brother was a brain in a jar. Sure, there were a lot more questions he wanted answered. But he felt like everything was going to be all right.

"Last one to the dorm is a Tuscan stink beetle!" Odifin cried when they got outside. He revved up his motor and zipped ahead through the jungle.

"Hey, wait up!" Newton yelled, and he raced after his strange half brother as the moon rose over the island. Whatever happened next, Newton was excited to have family to share it with.

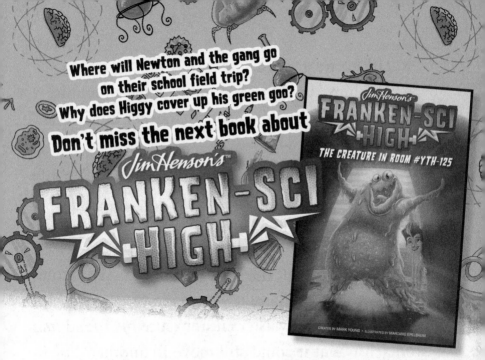

Where will Newton and the gang go on their school field trip?
Why does Higgy cover up his green goo?
Don't miss the next book about

Jim Henson's

FRANKEN-SCI HIGH

Jim Henson's

FRANKEN-SCI HIGH

THE CREATURE IN ROOM #YTH-125

CREATED BY MARK YOUNG • ILLUSTRATED BY MARIANO EPELBAUM

"Attention, students! Today our lunch staff accidentally used the recipe for interdimensional meatloaf instead of international meatloaf. If your meatloaf has disappeared from your plate unexpectedly, you may choose another lunch special."

The loud chatter in the Franken-Sci High cafeteria died down during the announcement, and rose again to a dull roar when it had finished.

Newton Warp looked down at the square of gray meat on his plate. He picked up his fork and attempted to stab the loaf, but it shimmered and disappeared because it could.

"Rats!" Newton cried.

Next to him Higgy, his roommate, burped loudly. "I ate mine before it could escape to another dimension," he said.

"How do you know it won't still escape?" Newton asked.

"What do you mean?" Higgy asked.

"Well, you might have absorbed it into your—your goo," Newton began. (He'd been going to say "stomach," but Higgy Vollington was made of green protoplasm, and Newton wasn't entirely sure his friend *had* a stomach.) "But it could still move to another dimension once it's inside you, right?"

"You may be right," Higgy agreed. "Then I'll just be hungry again! Better get something else to eat." He slid off the bench and made his way back to the lunch line, making a *pffft pffft pffft* sound as he moved.

Across the table Newton's friend Shelly Ravenholt pushed her plate toward him. "Want to share my salad?"

"That's okay," Newton replied. "I'm not that hungry anyway. Those protein pancakes at breakfast filled me up."

At the end of the table, a brain in a jar trained its eyeballs on Newton.

"I don't know why everybody makes such a fuss about eating," said Odifin Pinkwad. "It seems like such a bother. And you have to do it three times a day."

"Five," corrected Rotwang Conkell, a tall, skinny boy next to Odifin. His plate was piled with a mountain of nuggets.

The robot student sitting next to Shelly frowned. "Well, I don't eat either, but I'm glad we get a break three times a day," said Theremin Rozika. "Otherwise we'd just have three more classes."

"Didn't I hear that your dad was working on artificial taste buds, Theremin?" Shelly asked. "That would be cool. Then you could see what you're missing. You too, Odifin."

"I can assure you, I'm not missing anything," Odifin said.

Higgy came back and slapped a tray of purple gelatin onto the table. "It helps to be nice to the lunch ladies," Higgy said. "They gave me extra helpings!"

"They prefer to be called 'dining engineers,'" Shelly reminded him.

A feeling of happy calm came over Newton as he looked at all his friends.

Just a few months ago, Shelly and Theremin found me in the library Brain Bank, with no memory of who

I was or where I'd come from, Newton thought. *I thought I'd never fit in or find out what my story was. But now . . .*

But now Newton was closer than ever to learning the truth. First he and his friends had discovered that Newton had special abilities. He could instantly grow gills if he jumped into water. He could camouflage himself if he was in danger. He could change his appearance to mimic others. His sticky hands and feet allowed him to climb up walls and stick to ceilings. And he was discovering new things all the time.

Newton had done his best to keep those special abilities a secret. At the same time, he had tried to find out the truth about his past. Headmistress Mumtaz seemed nice, but whenever he questioned her, she'd say she couldn't tell Newton anything, which was strange. Then a mysterious green-haired man had started following him around. The man had turned out to be Professor Flubitus, who said he'd come from the future to protect Newton, because Newton was somehow—in a way he did not yet understand—very important to the future of the school.

This was interesting, but Newton didn't necessarily want to know about his future—he wanted to know about his past. Finally Flubitus had revealed that

Newton had a relative at Franken-Sci High. After an intense search, and some DNA testing, Newton had discovered who that relative was: Odifin the brain in a jar, was his half brother!

Newton gazed over at Odifin, who was talking to Rotwang. Odifin thought about what he wanted to say, and then his words came out of a speaker attached to his jar.

"I hear they're showing a movie called *The Thing with Two Heads* in the gym tonight," Odifin said to Rotwang. "We should go!" Then Odifin looked at Newton. "Want to come, Bro?"

"Thanks, Odifin, but I need to check my schedule," Newton replied. "I think I have a homework assignment to do."

Theremin's eyes flashed red. "'Bro'? Aren't you guys half brothers? Or is it more like *quarter* brothers?"

Newton heard an edge in his robot friend's voice, and suspected that Theremin was a little bit jealous about the fact that Newton and Odifin were brothers of any kind. Newton understood where Theremin was coming from. Until recently Odifin had been a rude, mean kid who wasn't particularly nice to Newton and his friends. Newton and Odifin had only become friendly right before the big news.

On the other hand, even though Newton and Theremin's friendship had gotten off to a rocky start, they'd already formed a stronger bond than Newton and Odifin. Newton guessed that Theremin's jealous side was showing through, and maybe this time it was for a good reason . . . .